The Nameless Ones

Short Story Collection

Mesu Andrews

Edutainment Ink

Copyright © 2024 by Mesu Andrews

All rights reserved.

No part of this book may be reproduced in any form or by any electronic or mechanical means, including information storage and retrieval systems, without written permission from the author, except for the use of brief quotations in a book review.

Published in the United States by Edutainment Ink.

Edutainment Ink Logo Designed by Stanford Campbell.

Cover Design by Amanda Geaney.

Cover Construction by Roseanna White.

ISBN 978-1-959706-11-3 (Trade paperback)

ISBN 978-1-959706-12-0 (Ebook)

Contents

Introduction v
Character Lists vii

The 700th Wife

Note to Reader 3
Chapter 1 5
Chapter 2 11
Chapter 3 15
Chapter 4 22
Chapter 5 28
Epilogue 35
Author's Note 37

The Water Girl

Note to Reader 43
Chapter 1 45
Chapter 2 49
Chapter 3 52
Chapter 4 56
Chapter 5 60
Chapter 6 66
Author's Note 71

The Mole's Wife

Note to Reader 75
Chapter 1 77
Chapter 2 82
Chapter 3 87

Chapter 4	94
Chapter 5	101
Chapter 6	105
Chapter 7	112
Chapter 8	118
Chapter 9	125
Authors Note	131
About the Author	135
Also by Mesu Andrews	137

Introduction

My writing life began in the late 1990's while studying *Women of the Bible by* Ann Spangler with a group of women at my local church. Intrigued by the chapter on Solomon's Song of Songs, I began reading that Book of the Bible every day for a year. Yep—all eight chapters, every day. At first, I didn't understand a single verse. After a few months, however, a sort of allegory unfolded. It then morphed into a Bible study, which twelve years later became the novel, *Love's Sacred Song* (Revell, 2012).

If you've read Solomon's Song of Songs, you know he writes about his "Beloved" but never names her. How could I have written an entire novel about a woman with no name? The key word is *novel*. I write FICTION, so I gave her a name with deep meaning: Arielah, Lion of God.

Though I use historical research with creative fiction to form a plot, every novel's firm foundation is always the absolute *Truth* of God's Word. The truth is—the Bible was written during a time and culture when women were devalued. They were traded and treated as little more than property. But the God of Abraham, Isaac, and Jacob moved in the hearts of the writers of Scripture to mention certain women in key parts of His story. Some women are listed by name, some by relation ship (mother of, sister of, etc.), while others are described by location or station in life (widow of Zarephath). Think how profound this decision was to include *women* in such an important historical record! The mere mention of a woman—named or unnamed—in a patriarchal record was like an exclamation point for every woman who heard that story read.

Shouldn't someone research and write about **The Nameless Ones**?

In the pages that follow, you'll read about three stories that give a voice to the obscure, forgotten, and/or nameless women who are fictional—but their *roles* in Old Testament history are very real. All three stories in three different eras of Israelite kings, will reveal one main theme: Though she be quiet, she be mighty. Each story explores a famous (or infamous) Old Testament king and proposes a fictional woman who might have been at work behind the scenes to affect an important biblical event. Meet King Solomon in his old age, King Ahab on Mt. Carmel, and King Hezekiah who desperately needs his best tunnel digger to finish his project before the Assyrians besiege Jerusalem!

For each of the three stories, you'll find a *Note to Reader* that introduces the context and an *Author's Note* at the end to explain the important distinctions between fiction, fact, and Biblical Truth. Happy Reading, my friend!

Character Lists

The 700th Wife

Abishag	Wife to Prince Nathan
Adria	Eliada's Maid
Ahijah	Yahweh's Chief Prophet
Eliada	The 700th Wife
Iddo	King's Bodyguard Commander
Nathan	Solomon's Brother
Shlomit	Nathan's & Abishag's Daughter
Solomon	King of Israel

The Water Girl

Ahab	King of Israel
Elijah	Prophet of God
Elika	Temple Cook
Jezebel	Queen of Israel
Miriam	The Water Girl
Obadiah	Palace Administrator
Rachel	The Water Girl's Sister
Tirzah	A Water Girl

The Mole's Wife

Bekira	Eliakim's Wife
Daniel	Judah's Mole
Eliakim	Chief Engineer/Palace Administrator
Hephzibah	Queen of Judah
Hezekiah	King of Judah
Jahleel	Eliakim's & Bekira's Son
Jerusha	The Mole's Wife
Levi	Mysterious Old Man

The 700th Wife

Note to Reader

Without reading farther than the title, *The 700th Wife,* do you know which of Israel's kings this story is about? Yep, Solomon. In *The 700th Wife,* you'll meet Solomon's last love. As mentioned in the introduction, Solomon's Song of Songs was the reason I started writing, and *Love's Sacred Song* told the story of his *first* love. Both stories are fiction but have been created to explain why he might have written both Song of Songs and Ecclesiastes—two of Scripture's wisdom Books with completely opposite tones.

If you've read *Love's Sacred Song,* you know the epilogue delivers a huge shocker. *The 700th Wife* builds on that surprise ending! If you haven't read *Love's Sacred Song and* would rather not see the spoiler, skip to the second story (or pick up a copy of *Love's Sacred Song* and read it first)!

Here's the good news: You need not have read *Love's Sacred Song* to understand *The 700th Wife!* The story you're about to read stands alone as a tribute to the brave young woman who was the last to enter Solomon's harem. I've imagined her as Eliada, daughter of Yahweh's chief prophet, Ahijah. Solomon believed giving her the inauspicious privilege of becoming his 700th wife would somehow keep Ahijah from stirring sedition in the northern tribes of Israel. But we discover that neither Eliada nor her abba care so deeply for this life *under the sun.*

When Solomon hears that phrase and sees the wisdom springing from this very young Yahweh follower, he enlists her help in recording his ramblings during a time that would normally have been their wedding week. What could possibly happen locked in a wedding chamber with an old king for eight days?

One

*"The words of the Teacher, son of David, king in Jerusalem:
'Meaningless! Meaningless!' says the Teacher. 'Utterly
meaningless! Everything is meaningless.' What do people gain
from all their labors at which they toil under the sun?"*
Ecclesiastes 1:1-3

Eliada

I waited patiently for my royal groom in his opulent chamber, feasting on the surroundings. A lavish private garden lay beyond the king's multi-roomed chamber, but I dared not make him search for me on our wedding night. Animals' stuffed heads covered the walls around me, staring down with ebony eyes. I shivered and tried to ignore them, digging my bare toes into the crimson-and-blue plush rug—the colors of royalty. Looking down at my plain, linen robe, I shook my head and wondered again how I got here.

King Solomon's chamber—his 700th wife.

The thought of it propelled me off the cushioned couch and toward the double-doored balcony overlooking the Kidron Valley. The view was stunning—except for the hideous altar to

Chemosh atop the Mount of Olives. Five days ago, I served stew to my abba and the other Yahweh prophets at Shiloh, living in the shadow of the Tabernacle. I felt God's presence though His Ark had been taken to Jerusalem before my birth. Rumors said Solomon gave it to Sheba's queen, but the prophets refused to believe it. I couldn't believe it. I must trust Yahweh's presence fills the Temple nearby so I can live in a harem filled with foreign women and their pagan gods.

I know my calling, Yahweh, and I will obey—even if it costs my life.

"There you are." A deep voice startled me, and I gasped, turning to see Israel's king at the balcony's threshold. Tall and broad-shouldered, he held out one hand as if steadying a skittish mare. "I didn't mean to frighten you. I'm sure this has all been very unsettling."

Unsettling? I wanted to rail at him. Instead, I nodded a respectful bow and then boldly met his appraisal. "I'm not frightened, my lord. I am your obedient servant. Do with me as you please." He had every right as my king and husband.

But when he started across the mosaic tiles, my courage faltered. With every step closer, I pressed my back harder against the balcony rail. In one fluid motion, his arm found my waist, and he pulled me against him. "I can't have a bride toppling off my balcony on our wedding day." A slight grin curved his lips. "Surely, becoming my wife isn't worth throwing yourself into the Kidron."

For an excruciating moment, I had no words. His dark-brown eyes appraised me, and I took in his salt-and-pepper hair, gold crown, and kind expression. His heartbeat raced beneath the hands I pressed on his chest—a heart no longer devoted to Yahweh.

I pushed him away. "Thank you for your concern, my king, but I assure you, I won't harm myself. I'm here in obedience to my abba and to Yahweh." I hurried into the chamber and walked straight to a curtained area, slipped past the sheers, and sat on his soft mattress. "May I assume since we had no betrothal or formal wedding," I fairly shouted while he dawdled at the balcony, "that we will also dispense with the wedding week and the feast?" The prophets' wives at Shiloh had prepared me for my wedding night.

Through the sheer fabric, I saw him leave the balcony and walk toward me, hands clasped behind his back. He approached as if strolling through a garden, but my nerves wound tighter as he came near.

You're being ridiculous, Eliada. I was sixteen, not a child. I'd faced hardship before. My ima had died giving me life, so Abba —Shiloh's chief prophet—raised me to confront adversity with Yahweh in my heart and a chip on my shoulder. Israel's king could take my body, but Yahweh alone held my heart.

The king pulled back a curtain with a single finger. My neck and face felt like they caught fire, and my tongue stuck to the roof of my mouth.

"I've encountered a vast array of women's emotions on a wedding night," he said, "but I must say I'm intrigued by your relative calm." He emerged through the curtains and climbed the two steps to his bed. Fluffed a few pillows. Flopped on his side. Propping his head on one hand, he said, "You mentioned obedience to Yahweh and your abba as your reasons for being here. How much of our agreement did Ahijah share with you?"

I heard the censure in his voice and stared at a king whose power reached into Egypt, Sidon, Ammon, Edom, Moab, and beyond. "If I tell you, will you try to have him killed as you did Jeroboam?"

His brows lifted, and a slow smile made him dangerously handsome. "So, you're beautiful *and* intelligent. Should a king not defend his throne against a man like Jeroboam who incites sedition?"

"My abba anointed Jeroboam at Yahweh's command. He *will* someday rule over ten of Israel's tribe."

His smile changed to clenched teeth. "What else have they told you in that prophets' camp?"

Was I signing Abba's death warrant by confiding my knowledge? But he'd told me to let honesty be my guide and Yahweh my Protector. I straightened my spine and rolled my shoulders back. "I know I'm your seven hundredth wife and that you have three hundred concubines. I know you've married women from the nations with which Yahweh specifically commanded Israel not to intermarry, and that both they and their gods have seduced you into idolatry. I also know Yahweh is raising up strong enemies against you."

The king shifted from his repose to sit beside me. He'd seemed less intimidating lying down. Now, towering over me, eyes narrowed, he was terrifying. "And what of our marriage, little Eliada? Did your abba tell you why I demanded to marry the daughter of Yahweh's chief prophet?"

I refused to look away. "He said you gave no reason, but Yahweh affirmed your request, so I am here—at your mercy." Emotion warbled my last word, and I turned away, ashamed of my weakness.

The king's finger curled around my chin, drawing my eyes back to his. "Since my reason for wanting you seems the only information you lack, let me tell you. Though I would never willingly harm you, Eliada, the Yahweh prophets have become a thorn in my sandal. With you a willing hostage in my harem, I suspect they'll think twice before anointing another king to steal my throne."

Now, it was my turn to smile. Even chuckle.

He released my chin. "Do I amuse you?"

"I'm willing but not a hostage, my king. The prophets—including my abba—knew that our goodbye could be the last time we spoke under the sun."

His expression was part shock, part fury. "An abba can't offer his only child to a king and just walk away. I have many daughters, and I would kill any man who threatened a single one of them."

"Then you have no understanding of how utterly meaningless this life is, King Solomon." His eyes rounded, but I continued before he could reply. "Your threats have no effect on me or Yahweh's prophets because nothing in this world is as glorious as the life that awaits us in Yahweh's presence."

Mouth agape, the king's silence unnerved me more than his threats. When he suddenly lifted his hand, I winced and waited for the blow. Instead, he reached for a bell and shouted, "Steward!" Then he sprang off the bed and began pacing. "Meaningless. Utterly meaningless. What do we gain from our endless toil?" He stopped and looked at me. "What was that phrase you used?"

"Your threats mean nothing—"

"No, no. When describing the last time you spoke to the prophets—our current state?" He circled his hand as if pulling the words from my lips with an invisible thread.

"Under the sun?"

"Yes, yes, that's it! Beautiful!" He clapped as the steward appeared, and the king whirled on him. "Bring me blank scrolls —many of them—with my reeds and pigments." The man scurried back through the door from which he'd come, and King Solomon returned his attention to me. "*Under the sun*—it describes the human condition. You are young, my little Eliada, but I find in you a deep well of wisdom." He knelt and cradled my hand in his own. "You will help me explain for my descendants how I've used the wisdom Yahweh gave me to build this kingdom, yet He still raised up enemies against me."

"I will not!" I said, pulling my hand away. "Will you blame Yahweh for your poor choices?" His small gasp and rounded eyes made him appear almost . . . vulnerable. He stood and turned his back but didn't walk away.

What am I to do with him, Yahweh? My heart softened toward this mere man who pleaded innocence to sins others saw so plainly. *Yahweh, give me Your love for the one You named Jedediah—beloved of the Lord—at his birth.*

I descended the elevated bed and walked around to face my husband and king. I rested my hands on the arms folded over his chest like a shield, but he refused to look at me. I whispered my plan anyway. "We will discover together how your God-given wisdom has been veiled to what truly matters, and we will write it down for your descendants who reign after you."

Two

"Daughters of Jerusalem, I charge you by the gazelles and by the does of the field: Do not arouse or awaken love until it so desires."
Song of Solomon 2:7

I had no idea that King Solomon would take my suggestion to examine his veiled wisdom so seriously. We'd been philosophizing and recording his thoughts on parchment for five days.

"Fools fold their hands and ruin themselves," he continued, stuffing the last piece of this morning's bread in his mouth. "Better to fill one hand peacefully than two hands with struggle and chasing after mist."

"Too fast!" I lifted my hand, halting his dictation. "Better . . . to fill . . . one hand . . ." I'd finished my morning meal quickly and started documenting each pearl that fell from his lips.

He smoothed a tendril of my hair behind one ear. "You don't even realize you're beautiful, do you, Eliada?"

I ignored the question. ". . . than two hands . . . with struggle . . . and chasing after mist." I looked up. "You may proceed."

Stretched out beside me on a crimson rug, he grinned. "There was a man all alone who had neither son nor brother. He never stopped working, Eliada. Why? For what purpose did he build wealth? Why deprive himself of pleasure?" His penetrating eyes unnerved me.

I looked down at my ink-stained hands. "Is that to be recorded, or are you asking my opinion?"

He sat up suddenly, took the stylus from my hand, and set it beside the parchment. "Enough of this," he whispered against my cheek. Drawing his finger gently down my neck, he paused at the base of my throat. "You've been my wife five days, and I haven't bedded you, little Eliada. Are you pleased or disappointed?"

My cheeks caught fire, and every muscle tensed. I'd waited each night for him to claim his husbandly rights, but I wrote until the moon rose high, and he always fell asleep before I joined him in bed.

"I won't force you, Eliada." He tilted his head to capture my down-turned eyes. "I respect you too much." An impish grin made him look younger, but I found the streaks of gray in his curly-dark hair quite handsome.

"You don't have to force me." The tremor in my voice betrayed me. I was no seductress, but I'd prepared for this. "May I freshen up first?"

"Of course." He brushed his lips across mine, soft as a butterfly's wings. "I'll send in a maid, and you can ring the bell for my steward when she's finished." He stood and lingered over me, offering his hand. "I'll be back as soon as you're ready."

I nodded, unable to speak past the lump in my throat. Did his heart truly *feel* the emotion his eyes expressed? Or was he simply charming? Watching him cross the chamber with long, powerful strides, I felt giddy. Had his 699 other wives felt the same way? Or his three hundred concubines? I could barely fathom the numbers. The attachments. Or the unattachment when they were banished to the harem to wait their turn.

In the quick preparation for my wedding, Abba and the prophets' wives told me of Solomon's women. "They're trade agreements," Abba said, looking distinctly uncomfortable before hurrying outside and leaving the details to the women.

"Most are treaty brides," Talmon's wife said, the youngest prophet's wife. "Daughters of kings and nobles given to Solomon as gifts to ensure peace within Israel's tribes and with surrounding nations."

If each of them had been given to seal a pact—like I'd been taken to secure Abba's loyalty—had Solomon ever known true affection? Had King Solomon been as tender with his other women as he was with me? Did any of them know—or care—that he was *Jedidiah*? That he was *loved by God,* named by Yahweh through the prophet Nathan?

Could I love him for the man I'd come to know these past five days? Though he was much older, I found him handsome. My heartbeat quickened until my conscience whispered. *He isn't devoted to Yahweh.* I could never truly share my heart with someone who didn't fully embrace the one, true God.

"Good morning, Mistress." I jumped at the voice of a girl who appeared younger than me. "Forgive me for startling you. I was told to prepare you for your wedding night." She stood holding a pitcher and towel.

Mortified, I wondered how soon before the whole palace knew I'd failed for five days to fulfill my marital duties to Israel's prolific king. "Yes, uh . . . thank you." Without a moment's hesitation, she set aside her tools and started to disrobe me. "Wait!" I said, stepping away. "What's your name?"

She giggled. "My name is Adria, and you need not be shy. I've prepared the last twenty of the king's brides." The girl's hands moved almost as quickly as a bee's wings. She washed, lotioned, massaged, painted, and deemed me *ready* for Israel's king by mid-afternoon. Amid all the primping we'd forgotten to eat, and my stomach growled like one of the beasts in the king's collection. "Well, we certainly can't have that happen when the king takes his favorite wife to bed. I'll bring you a light meal before—"

"Favorite wife?" I halted her. "Do you say that to all the women you prepare for him?"

The skin between her brows creased. "No. I usually don't talk at all to the others."

"Then why would you say such a thing to me?"

She walked over to peruse the scrolls and writing utensils. Reaching out to touch the parchment I'd been writing, she suddenly halted and looked at me. "May I touch it?"

"Of course—if you answer my question. Why did you say I was his favorite wife?"

She lightly brushed her fingers over the parchment. "My ima has served in the palace since the king's first year, and he's never let a wife record his wisdom."

Feeling suddenly self-conscious, I asked, "How did your ima know what we were doing in this chamber?"

Adria's head snapped toward me. "I didn't . . . I mean . . . Please, Mistress. Don't tell the king. My abba is his steward, and he told ima. He said it's been years since the king was this happy."

I closed the distance between us. "I won't tell, Adria, and I don't know what our lives will be like after . . ." My cheeks warmed, but I forged ahead. "When the king sends me to the harem, is it possible I could see you again?"

She nodded and offered a tentative smile. "Anything is possible for the king's new wife. You need only make your wishes known, and I would be honored to serve you." After a slight bow, she added, "I'll let Abba know you're ready for the king's return." I watched the girl go, feeling as though I had at least one friend in Solomon's palace.

Three

"Let him kiss me with the kisses of his mouth—for your love is more delightful than wine."
Song of Solomon 1:2

After Adria left, I stood before the king's full-length bronze mirror assessing my reflection. I wore a plain blue linen robe with an embroidered belt. My hair hung loose in dark curls past my waist, and my only jewelry was an emerald pendant—serving as my dowry. A prophet had little earthly wealth to offer his daughter, even one marrying a king. The gem felt odd hanging from my neck. I lifted it to look closer, and it caught the afternoon sun, casting lovely reflections on the wall.

How much longer before Solomon returned?

I decided to organize my writing table, gathering the pigments and writing utensils together. I then skimmed the parchments for content and put them in some sort of order as I rolled them and set them in groupings. The weight of Adria's words rested heavily on me as I worked. Why had Solomon allowed me to share in his wisdom? I'd even dared question him, challenging some of his doubt and pessimism. Who was I to dispute the wisest king in the world? A man endowed with Yahweh's divine gift?

His reaction was more than tolerant. I thought at first I was merely an amusement, but as the days passed, I'd come to see true humility in the king I'd married.

I ran my fingers over what I'd written on one parchment: *The king said to himself, "Come now, I will test you with pleasure to find out what is good." But that also proved meaningless.* On another parchment: *I denied myself nothing I desired and refused nothing enticing. My heart took great pleasure in every project, each one its own reward. Yet when I surveyed all my accomplishments, everything I'd struggled to achieve, it was all meaningless. Chasing after the wind. I'd gained nothing under the sun.*

I secured both parchments with leather ties and placed them in the *pleasure* pile—quite a large one—all the while considering Solomon's vast life experience. He'd known women of every size, shape, and color. Faced countless kings and queens, demanding tribute, receiving gifts, gaining respect.

My palms suddenly grew sweaty. I glanced at his chamber doors. What could I offer such a man? I knew nothing of pleasing him. Nothing of building temples and palaces. Very little about the nations with which he'd maintained peace for the nearly forty years of his reign.

My heart pounded like a drum. No longer the ardent expectation of our intimate encounter, now the fear of inadequacy beat down my anticipation. The door latch clicked, and I felt like a doe in a hunter's cross-hairs. A gasp escaped the moment I saw him in his gold crown, fox-fur collar, and floor-length purple cape.

"I hope you weren't waiting too long," he said, removing the finery as he strode to his wardrobe. "Makeda's son returned to Jerusalem today. I couldn't believe it. Why would he come—today of all days?"

I had no idea what he was talking about. "Who is Makeda?"

His hand stilled on the cabinet door before closing it gently. When he turned toward me, he wore only a white linen robe with a jeweled belt. His expression betrayed his unease. "I shouldn't bore you with court business." He took a step toward me.

"Please tell me!" I blurted. "Who is Makeda?"

His eyes widened—then softened with smile lines at each corner. "Come, little one. We should talk a bit. I can see you're nervous." He offered his hand and led me to his elevated bed, pushing aside doeskin pillows. Patting the lion-skin blanket, he coaxed me to lie beside him. I sat stiffly on the side of the bed while he began. "Makeda is the Queen of Sheba, and she says her son, Menelik, is *my* son."

I felt the blood drain from my face. "It's rumored you gave her the Ark *and* a son."

A low chuckle rumbled in his chest. "I didn't give her either."

"I knew it. I knew you wouldn't—"

"I could have given her a son, Eliada." He held my gaze, making his meaning clear.

I looked away, hoping he didn't see my revulsion. He'd bedded the Queen of Sheba but didn't marry her. Did he take his pleasure with every woman who visited his palace? "How can you be sure he's not your son?"

"I sent spies with Makeda's caravan when she left Jerusalem. Ten months later, she gave birth to a healthy but small baby boy."

His report was so matter-of-fact, I looked at him again. "But he thinks he's your son. Doesn't he deserve to know the truth?"

He laid back, looking at the ceiling. "I asked Menelik to stay in Jerusalem, hoping after spending time with him, I could tell him. Honestly, he'd make a better king than my firstborn, Rehoboam. But Menelik doesn't have David's blood in his veins. He can never rule Israel."

I leaned over him. "Will he stay?"

"No." Profound sadness surrounded that simple word. "We spent the day together, and he decided to leave. Aagh! It's not important right now." Before I could assure him it was important, he'd pulled me close, rolled me on my back, and was hovering over me with a mischievous smile. "This is what's important now. I've looked forward to being with you all day."

Staring into his midnight eyes, I so badly wanted to believe him. "Why?"

He grinned. "Perhaps after we've shared the fruit of marriage, you'll understand."

"No—" I sighed, wondering if my cheeks would permanently be aflame in his presence. "I mean why *me*? Why did you allow me to write down your wisdom?"

Sobering, he traced his finger across my forehead. "You are intelligent, Eliada, but more than that. You apply knowledge with discernment. Not everyone possesses such a gift—especially at such a young age. Even fewer pair the gift with such beauty." He brushed his lips across mine. "You are a rare find, and I treasure you."

In that moment, I believed. I believed he thought me special, that perhaps out of a thousand women, I could be his favorite. Through his tenderness, I learned desire. Through his patience, I learned pleasure. And because of his kindness, I even believed Yahweh could redeem his heart. The next morning, we woke in each other's arms, and I knew without a doubt that I loved Solomon ben David, King of Israel.

For the next three days, we lived in the protective cocoon of his chamber, continuing the wisdom writing we'd begun. Though still somewhat pessimistic, he'd begun to insert glimpses of hope. Glimpses of Yahweh's redemption in his gloomy reports of meaninglessness under the sun.

When the moon rose on that third night, I set aside the stylus and stretched my hand. "How will you know we're finished with it?"

"Why?" He stopped pacing and cast an impish grin over his shoulder. "Getting bored?"

"Not bored. I just wonder how you'll know you've said enough—finished your struggle *under the sun*."

The right side of his mouth quirked strangely, and his eyes narrowed as if pondering. "There's really no end of making of books, and I think too much study wearies the body." He walked over to my low table and knelt beside me. "We'll decide on the order of the scrolls later, but here are my final words. 'Now all has been heard, and here is the conclusion: Fear Yahweh and keep His commandments because this alone is the duty of mankind. For Yahweh will bring every deed into . . . judge . . . incruding ery . . . "

"Solomon?" I turned to see him rubbing the right side of his face.

"Wheer . . . good or—" He sat with a jolt, looking dazed.

"Solomon!" I shook his shoulders. "Solomon talk to—"

He fell sideways, eyes distant and staring, like he couldn't hear or see me.

"Help! Help us! Help the king!" Wrapping my arms around his neck, I whispered, "You can't die. I've just started loving you."

Rough hands pulled me off, dragging me away. Someone spoke, but I knew only Solomon, lying on the floor. His eyes empty but blinking. Drool escaped one corner of his mouth. His chamber guards around him didn't wipe it away. Solomon would be mortified.

"Help him!" I lunged forward but strong hands gripped my arm.

"I said tell me what happened, or I'll question you in the prison."

Suddenly aware of the guard beside me, I bristled at his tone. "I'm his wife! Why would I hurt—"

"You wouldn't be the first to try to poison him."

"Poison—" Horrified, I looked back at Solomon. He

couldn't verify the truth I was about to tell. "The king was dictating the last couplet, but his words became garbled and he —" I shook my head, emotions choking my defense.

The guard's grip loosened as he scanned the scrolls littering the king's chamber. "So you're the one," he said, now measuring me with curiosity. "My men and I have noticed the king's improved disposition and believed the cause related to his new wife."

Was I to feel honored or angry that I was the subject of all palace gossip? "So you believe me?"

"I—" The physician rushed in, and I stood aside while the guard relayed my account of events to the king's doctor.

"Get him on the bed." Six guards lifted my husband, carrying him to the bed, while the physician unpacked his basket of small clay pots and jars.

The king's steward touched my hand gently, making me jump. "Forgive me, my lady, but can I bring you anything? Watered wine, perhaps?"

I shook my head, unable to speak past the emotions choking me. The physician shouted orders at the guards as if he were their commander. "I want the three other palace doctors here to consult."

The guard who seized me seemed to be their leader. He sent three men for the physicians and doled out orders to two others. "Secure this chamber so no one except we six come in or go out. Summon the royal council to determine if or when we tell anyone outside the palace." He pinned the king's steward with a dangerous stare. "Make sure none of the servants get wind of this. The fewer who know, the better."

The steward bowed. "Of course, my lord." He moved to the king's bedside, following the physician's quiet instruction.

Evidently, I'd become invisible. What was I to do? Where was I to go? Solomon had promised to personally escort me to the harem when we finished the book. He wanted to tell me which of his women were "safe" and which were likely to be unkind. Dreading the exile I knew would come, I began arranging the scrolls on my table, hoping to put off the inevitable.

My captor cleared his throat behind me. "Excuse me, Mistress."

I straightened but didn't face him, already blinking away tears. "Yes?"

"I should escort you to the harem now. The physician said the king may not wake for days."

"Days?" I whirled on him. "But he was fine—"

"Mistress, you cannot stay in the king's chamber."

"I understand, but Solomon wanted to take me to the harem himself. As a follower of Yahweh—and as the wife who was with the king when he fell ill—I won't be received well among his pagan wives." I couldn't hide my tears, and I felt myself losing control. Falling on one knee, I placed the man's hand against my forehead. "Please, take me somewhere else. I won't be any trouble. Or you could take me back to Shiloh, to the prophet's camp until the king recovers."

"Mistress, stand," he said, removing his hand from mine. "I don't know—"

"Please. Please!" I said as he pulled me to my feet. "I could take a servant girl with me to someone's home—Adria, the steward's daughter. I wouldn't be any trouble at all. Surely, there's someone in Jerusalem who's faithful to Yahweh and wouldn't hate me for loving our king."

The man's features softened, and his pause gave me hope. A little gasp fueled a spark of something promising. "I know exactly where I'll take you, Mistress, but you won't need a maid."

Four

*"When King David was very old, he could not keep warm even when they put covers over him... Then they searched throughout Israel for a beautiful young woman and found Abishag, a Shunammite, and brought her to the king...
she took care of the king and waited on him,
but the king had no sexual relations with her."*
1 Kings 1:1, 3-4

Solomon's guard led me out of the palace and through the streets of the Upper City. My captor became my guide, greeting every soldier we passed with a nod. They, however, stood at strict attention, slamming fists against their breastplates, when they saw him approach.

"May I know your name?" I asked. "Or at least why the guards salute you?"

He almost smiled. "I am Iddo, commander of the king's bodyguard."

The bruises where he'd gripped my arm still ached. "I suppose that explains your zeal for my husband's welfare."

No response, his eyes forward.

I missed my maid, Adria, already. She'd served our morning

meal each day, and I'd hoped she could be my companion in exile. *Yahweh, help me to be thankful to be anywhere but the harem.*

My guide turned down a quiet street, the western palace wall on one side, a row of extravagant stone houses with elegant gardens on the other. Though relieved he hadn't taken me to prison, I'd feel just as tortured in a stuffy noblemen's house.

"Where are you taking me?"

He halted beside a towering iron gate, where two more guards saluted him. Iddo ignored them, turning to me with his voice low. "You'll be safe with the king's brother and his wife, Mistress, but you must let me explain the situation. Do you understand?"

"The king's bro—" Why would he bring me here? A thousand more questions raced through my mind. I didn't know Iddo or the king's family, but something in this man's countenance made me trust him. Only one question mattered. "Do they worship Yahweh?"

A grin brightened his features. "Yes—as do I."

The gate swung open, and we entered a glorious courtyard filled with fruit trees, plants, and flowering shrubs. I followed Iddo but wished I could stroll through the lush sanctuary and forget that my husband was gravely ill in the palace behind me. *Will I ever see you again, Solomon?* The thought brought a rush of emotion I hadn't expected.

"Iddo, welcome!" A stunning, willowy woman approached us, subtle gray curls peeking out from her head covering. I swiped at errant tears but not before she noticed. "Who is this wilted flower you've brought me?" The elegance with which she moved was breathtaking. The air barely stirred.

"Shalom, Mistress Abishag." Iddo bowed, and I did the same. He gave me a sideways glance, and I realized as wife of the king, I need not bow to anyone but Solomon. Flustered, I clasped my hands to keep from fidgeting.

"This is Eliada," Iddo said. "We bring sad news. Is Prince Nathan at home?"

"He's inside." Even stricken, she was lovely. "Follow me."

We left the courtyard's earthy beauty to find Abishag's home very similar. A tree stretched up through the entryway roof. Greenery and flowering plants sat beneath every window.

"Nathan!" She led us through a large gathering room, down a hall, and into a room where scrolls filled shelves on every wall. "Nathan, my love, Iddo brings news of your brother."

The man seated at the low table looked up with eyes like Solomon's. His hair was lighter brown and not as gray, but I saw the same strong jaw line and chiseled cheekbones that made my husband so handsome.

Prince Nathan set aside his scroll but didn't look up. "What's Solomon done this time?" The mirth in his tone fled when he stood and saw the guard's face—and me standing beside him. "What happened, Iddo? Who is this?"

"The king had an *episode* while dictating to his new wife. The physician is with him now to assess why his speech became garbled." Nodding at me, he added, "This is Eliada, daughter of Abijah the prophet, your brother's seven-hundredth wife."

An uneasy glance passed between the prince and his wife. "I recall making their marriage arrangement, but why—"

"She's been with the king since their wedding day—nearly two weeks—and he's dictated a book of wisdom to her. He's changed." He stepped closer to Nathan. "Eliada worships Yahweh, my prince. You know her fate if she goes to the harem."

"You want her to stay here?" Nathan's eyes grew as wide as camel's hooves. "She can't—"

"I think you men should talk privately," Abishag interrupted. "Eliada and I will tour the courtyard."

I wanted to find a cave and hide. Head down and eyes averted, I followed the woman from the prince's library to the peaceful place we first met. The silence during the walk grew awkward, but I didn't know what to say. Though I couldn't bear the thought of the harem, I wouldn't beg to stay.

"Would you like to sit down?" she asked, motioning me toward a stone bench.

"Thank you." I realized it was much like the one I'd seen in Solomon's private garden and said so.

"Yes, Solomon's bench belonged to my dearest friend—his one, true love." Lifting her gaze to meet mine, she grinned. "But palace whispers say the king has fallen in love with you. Is that true?"

Heat surged into my neck and cheeks. "I, um . . . well, I . . ."

She cradled my hands. "Nothing would please me more, Eliada, because it would mean he's made peace with Yahweh."

"What do you mean?" Suddenly more confused than embarrassed, I set aside my insecurities. "Are you saying the king worshipped pagan gods because he was angry with Yahweh?"

"I don't know," she said, releasing my hands and tilting her face to the sunshine. "Who can understand the thoughts of a king given God's divine wisdom? But I believe he's searched his whole life to replace Arielah and found nothing to fill the void her death left."

Meaningless! Meaningless! So much of the book he'd dictated to me suddenly made sense. And the ending he tried to speak . . .

"Perhaps he is making peace with Yahweh," I said, hoping it was true. "On the day he signed the marriage contract, he seemed to feel rather confused—almost betrayed—by Yahweh. But as Solomon dictated his book of wisdom day after day, I believe he finally reached a conclusion that brought Yahweh into clearer focus."

She turned to me then, her gaze probing. "And you, Eliada? What conclusions have you reached after nearly two weeks with Israel's king?"

Pausing, I searched my heart before answering. What did I want life to look like—If Solomon lived? If he died? "The last two weeks have been the most fulfilling of my life. If Yahweh gives me more time with Solomon, I hope to somehow reconstruct those final words lost to his illness. I think they'll not only instruct future generations, but also heal his heart."

Abishag's perfect brows lifted. "I hope someday I get to read them." Sobering, concern etched her features. "How bad is he?"

Instant tears clogged my throat. I could only shake my head, fear stealing my words.

She pulled me into a fierce hug. "He's a fighter, you know. His name means *peace,* but he's strong. I can't imagine that Yahweh is finished with King Solomon."

"Ima?" A timid voice came from behind us and startled Abishag.

She released me as if I carried the plague. "Shlomit, my dove."

"Did I hear you say something happened to . . ." Shlomit looked at me warily. ". . . to King Solomon."

Abishag stood, towering over her daughter. They looked nothing alike. "Your . . . King Solomon has taken ill. This is Eliada, one of his wives. She was with him when—" Shlomit's eyes rounded, and she turned and ran like a frightened deer.

Abishag said nothing as she watched her go.

Strange. I stood and laid my hand on her shoulder. "Abishag?"

"Shlomit is the reason Nathan didn't want you here," she said without turning. "When my friend Arielah died, I promised I'd raise her daughter as my own. Solomon was so broken, he blamed the child for his wife's death and never asked what happened to her. He still doesn't know. We can't risk telling him." She faced me then, tears streaming down her cheeks. "Solomon is Nathan's brother, but he is a king *first,* which means he takes what he wants when he wants it. He can't take my Shlomit. She's married and has two children who need her. *I* need her."

Pulling this woman into my arms, I tried to reassure her as fiercely as she'd comforted me. "I will never speak of *your* daughter to Solomon. I vow it."

Footsteps approached, and we released each other, straightening our robes and wiping tears. Iddo and the prince approached, both wearing scowls.

"I must escort you to the harem," Iddo said.

"She's staying." Abishag wrapped her arm around my waist, standing beside me like a wall.

Her husband looked as if a strong wind might topple him. "She can't. You know—"

"All is well, husband. She stays." The elegant willow had become a strong oak, and—to my surprise—Prince Nathan's stern features softened to a grin.

He clapped Iddo's shoulder while gazing at his wife. "Abishag seldom forces her will, but when it happens, I've learned to trust her." Taking three more steps, he reached for my hand and pressed it to his forehead. "Welcome to our home, Eliada—King Solomon's seven-hundredth wife."

Five

"As for the other events of Solomon's reign—all he did and the wisdom he displayed—are they not written in the book of the annals of Solomon? Solomon reigned in Jerusalem over all Israel forty years."
1 Kings 11:41-42

I'd been in Nathan and Abishag's lovely home for three days. The prince had warmed the moment he saw I'd won his wife's approval. She was a mighty force, this beauty who spoke softly and exuded kindness.

Though Shlomit was slower to accept my friendship, by my third day in her parents' home, she seemed eager to know more about the king who sired her. "I've seen him, of course. Many times," she said, picking at a thread on her sleeve while Abishag played with the children. "But I've never been in the same room with him to study his mannerisms. His voice. His personality. Is he very much like Abba Nathan?"

"Since I've only known Prince Nathan for a few days, I can't say for sure." New to this royal family, I felt the need for caution. "Solomon loves to laugh, and your abba shows the same mischievous sense of humor. From the appearance of Nathan's library, I'd say both brothers love to learn." She nodded, her smile thoughtful. It was my turn to ask a question. "How could you live so close to the palace and never be discovered by the king?"

If a face had walls and a gate, Shlomit's slammed shut. "King Solomon has never stepped a sandal in our home. Abba was always summoned to the palace, and he hasn't seen Ima since the day I was born. She says her presence reminds the king too much of my birth ima, Arielah. Both women came from the north, the city of Shunem."

"I see." And I did—the pain on her features was palpable. It reminded me of the young man Menelik, who believed Solomon to be his abba because of the lie his Sheban queen mother told him. My husband's choices had broken many lives, but he'd been broken by them too. "King Solomon may be the wealthiest king on earth, but he's poorer for not knowing you, Shlomit."

Eyes moist, she hugged me. "Thank you, Eliada." Calling her children over, she thanked her ima for introducing us and started toward their neighboring home.

Abishag and I stood side-by-side, waving goodbye. "I want to see him today," I said.

My friend knew what I meant. "Nathan doesn't think—"

"I don't care," I said, turning toward her. "I'm going, with or without an escort."

"We should talk to Nathan." Taking me by the hand, she led me toward the house.

Each time I'd asked for an escort to visit my husband, Nathan had invented another excuse to keep me away—at least that's how it seemed. We arrived at the library doorway but didn't cross the threshold, waiting for him to look up.

Abishag squeezed my hand, her signal that I should speak. "Why won't you arrange an escort for me, Nathan? Is he dying?"

"Come in." He set aside his scroll with a deep sigh. "Sit down, both of you."

I hurried in, sitting on a cushion across from him, Abishag beside me.

"He's not recovering as quickly as the physicians hoped." Nathan scrubbed his face and sighed before looking at me intently. "He doesn't want to see you, Eliada. I think he's embarrassed by his weakness. He's quite changed from the man you saw three days ago."

"But I was with him when it happened. I saw him fall. I saw him drooling."

"He was mercifully spared that memory." Nathan's sad smile held compassion. "A man doesn't want the woman he loves to see him in such a state."

"Did he say he loved me?" My heart flipped over in my chest.

"He didn't need to. I haven't seen him this obsessed with a woman since—"

"Since Arielah?" Abishag's eyes sparkled. "Does he speak of Yahweh?"

Nathan rubbed at the ink stains on his hands. "He speaks of the book he and Eliada were writing and laments the last phrase he can't remember. He's sure it was about Yahw—"

"I'm the only one that can help him remember, Nathan." I stood abruptly, nearly upsetting the table, and was halfway to the door before the prince shouted.

"Wait! You can't go without an escort."

Abishag's smirk fueled my determination. "Then find me an escort, Prince Nathan—now."

Iddo was at Solomon's chamber door as Nathan and I traversed the mosaic tiles in the king's private hallway. The guard's memorably kind features became a frown as we drew near. "I'm sorry, my prince, but the king was clear. He will not see anyone but you and his physicians."

I stepped in front of Nathan. "I called for the guards on the day it happened, Iddo. I saw him, remember?"

"I remember."

"Does my husband look worse than that day?"

He hesitated; then lowered his voice. "He's no better."

I leaned forward, keeping my voice hushed too. "I've seen him at his worst, Iddo; and in our two weeks of marriage, I've seen the most vulnerable corners of his heart." I squared my shoulders. "Now, open the door. I will comfort my husband today."

He lifted a single brow, looking at Nathan, then opened the door and stepped out of the way. He whispered as I passed. "You may be the potion he needs."

We entered a chamber dark and stifling. Tapestries covered every window, and the odor of illness mingled with the burning oil lamps in wall niches. I covered my nose with a cloth I kept tucked in my belt. Worse yet was the terrible humming noise. I squinted, scanning the room for its source.

"It's the priests and necromancers," Nathan whispered. "Solomon's wives sent them to heal him."

Horrified, I said, "Does the king want them here?"

"No. He allows them in the outer rooms only. He can neither refuse their chanting nor let the priests see his weakness for fear they'll report to his wives and reap their ire."

"Israel's king will not be a captive in his own chamber. All of you, get out!" I shouted, and the whole chamber fell silent. "Out, I said! Get out!" I flew at the priests like a mother hen flogging a fox. "Let it be known that Israel's king worships Yahweh alone. Yahweh alone!" At least ten pompous pagans waddled from dark corners.

I scoured the room for stragglers but found only Iddo standing in the main chamber, eyes wide as full moons. "You've stirred up a hornets' nest, Mistress. They'll report to the harem, and the wives will—"

"The harem neither commands Israel's king, nor will he bow to their gods." I marched past the guard to slide back the tapestries on every window. "Iddo, please ask someone to open the shutters on these windows and open the balcony tapestries as well. How can Solomon recover in such darkness and gloom?"

Without waiting for his answer, I started toward my husband's bed chamber. Four physicians stared at me with wide-eyed dread. "He's asked not to be disturbed," one man ventured.

I turned to the bed, heavily veiled, and saw only a shadow. Shoulders propped up to a seated position on the feather-stuffed mattress, my husband was watching. "Don't come cwosuh." His voice was reedy and weak. "Pweav."

Tears burned my eyes. "But I love you." A sob escaped. I covered my mouth, trying to regain control.

"Don't."

"Don't love you? Too late. I already do." I sniffed, regaining composure. "So what do we do now?" I took a few more steps toward the curtains.

"Yeave, Elwee--aaahhh!" Frustrated, he threw a doe-skin pillow that landed against a curtain, pushing it open just a little.

Our eyes met. He looked like a frightened child, and my heart broke. "I like you calling me *Elie*." I climbed the elevated platform and sat on the end of his bed, boldly holding his gaze. "I'm not leaving you. I love you."

King Solomon squeezed his eyes closed and turned his face so I couldn't see the right side. He wore a stained purple robe and was covered with a smelly linen sheet. They'd shaved off his beard, and his hair looked like it hadn't been combed since the day I left. Drool ran down his chin.

"Iddo!" he shouted. "Take her."

"Iddo is busy," I said gently. "I asked him to brighten up

your chamber." Mustering my most intimidating glare, I addressed his physicians. "You may leave. All of you. King Solomon and I have work to do. He can summon you when we're finished."

They looked at me as if I were a cockroach and then at Solomon for his approval. He said nothing. Did nothing.

"I said, go!" I stood, hoping to be more intimidating. I wasn't elegant or soft-toned like Abishag, but I would have my way. All four royal physicians fled. When the chamber door clicked behind them, I climbed onto the bed and sat astride my husband as if riding a horse. "Did you hear? We have work to do, my king."

Palsy forgotten, he turned his shocked expression fully toward me. I wiped his chin with the cloth from my belt and kissed him thoroughly. At first, his arms hung at his sides, and I feared overestimating my effect on him. But before the thought curtailed my attempt, his left arm circled my waist, and my husband rolled me onto my back.

Propped on his left elbow, his right arm hung limp, but he hovered over me with searching eyes. "Why did you come?"

"I've told you. Because I love you." I pressed my cloth to the corner of his mouth, cradling his chin to lessen his embarrassment. "And because we must finish the last lines of your book. I'd like to know how your wisdom interprets the events of the past few days."

His arm began to tremble, unable to hold his weight. He fell to his side with a heavy sigh. "My wisdom says I hab become a weakwing. Wess dan a man."

I sat up, leaning over him now. "You are neither less than nor more than a man. You are *Jedidiah*, loved by God—and loved by me. Don't ever forget it." His mouth opened, but gathering tears seemed to steal his words. I kissed him gently this time. "We're going to clean you up and change your robe. By the end of this day, you'll feel more like yourself."

Without waiting for his protests, I scooted off the bed and

rang for fresh water and towels. The king's steward brought me the requested items and helped undress him.

"You may go," I said.

The man looked as if I'd slapped him. "But you'll need help with—"

"I'm quite capable. I'll ring again when we need you to take away the soiled linens." The steward looked to Solomon for help, but found none. "Yes, Mistress."

The moment the door clicked shut behind him, Solomon asked, "How can you wuv me?" He'd avoided my eyes since the steward arrived.

I wrung out the cloth and gently washed his face, drawing his chin upward so he'd look at me. "I love you because you showed me your heart, and now I know you're more than wisdom or wealth or power. You aren't *King* Solomon to me. You are Yahweh's Jedidiah."

A sob escaped, and he pressed his face against me, wrapping my waist with his left arm again. The sweetness of our afternoon—the hard truths of his limitations and the tender mercies of his love—were like spring rain on my parched heart.

"Are you ready to discuss the book's ending?" I asked, lying next to him.

"Mm-hmm. But I don't eemember."

"I remember. You said that fearing Yahweh and keeping His commands were the only duties of mankind because . . . " I sat up and held his gaze. "That's when your words became garbled. I couldn't understand the rest. Can you rem—"

"For Yahweh wiuh bwing ewery deed innoo ju . . . juzzhh—aahh." He growled and scrubbed his face. "I can't say it."

"But we can write it." I pulled his hands away, kissing each palm. "We can record it for future generations—together."

Epilogue

"Of making many books there is no end, and much study wearies the body.

Now all has been heard; here is the conclusion of the matter:

Fear God and keep his commandments, for this is the duty of all mankind.

For God will bring every deed into judgment, including every hidden thing, whether it is good or evil."

Ecclesiastes 12:12b-14

Author's Note

Here's the question that drove me to study both Ecclesiastes and Song of Songs:

How did Solomon depict such deep love for a woman in Song of Songs—but end up with 700 wives and 300 concubines?

Now for the question that drove me to write *The 700th Wife*:

How could Solomon write the most incredible love poem and then write Ecclesiastes—arguably, the most depressing book in the Bible?

I hope the combination of Biblical Truth, historical fact, and creative fiction has helped answer some of your questions about Israel's enigmatic, wise king.

What's Truth, Fact & Fiction?

Truth: Ahijah the Prophet

Unlike most of my books and short stories, *The 700th Wife* is **mostly** fiction. However, the story's foundational truth of Ahijah as a prophet and the coming unrest of the northern ten tribes against Judah is taken directly from Scripture. 1 Kings 11 tells us Ahijah prophesied that Israel would be torn apart. He then anointed Jeroboam as king of the northern ten tribes.

Fiction: Ahijah's Daughter

There is no Biblical record of Ahijah having a daughter or any sort of contact between him and Solomon. Nor does Scripture record any prophet or priest condemning King Solomon's idolatry (though the Bible clearly states his many wives led him to worship other gods: 1 Kings 11:4). Why wouldn't God's prophet(s) denounce Solomon's sin publicly? Perhaps the king's God-given wisdom was too intimidating, or his public-approval rating was too high for the prophets to chance it. This explanation seems unlikely since later prophets cared very little about public perception.

Could it be that God allowed Solomon's sin to go *publicly* unchallenged so He could privately deal with the man He'd named *Jedediah* (loved by God)? Then Solomon's private ponderings, thoughts, and wisdom were written down to bless generations. Aren't God's ways always higher and more glorious than ours?

Facts/Legends: Queen of Sheba

The snippet about the Queen of Sheba and her son is based on various and conflicting legends. 1 Kings 10:13 says Solomon gave her "all she desired," which some scholars have interpreted as meaning a baby *and* the Ark from the Temple. To me, it's a stretch, but it's an intriguing thought.

Truth: Nathan and Abishag

Nathan was indeed the king's brother and listed in 2 Samuel 5:14 as closest to Solomon in age. Abishag is also a biblical character (1 Kings 1) who we hear of only at David's death and Solomon's ascension to Israel's throne. There are legends in rabbinic literature about her role in Jewish history but nothing widely agreed on for Shunem's beauty queen.

Fiction: Shlomit

What about Shlomit? Sorry, she's *all* fiction. But the idea for Solomon's daughter was spurred by 1 Kings 4:11, in which one of Solomon's twelve governors is listed as "married to Taphath, daughter of Solomon." What if he gave preferential treatment to the daughters he wanted to keep close to home? I chose to keep Arielah's daughter secret from Solomon (as you read about in the epilogue of *Love's Sacred Song*) but gave *Shlomit* a name similar to her dad's, with the same meaning (peace).

The Water Girl

Note to Reader

I hope you enjoyed my researched imaginings of what Solomon's last weeks on earth might have been like. If you'd like to check out a fairly accurate and comprehensive Old Testament timeline, Biblehub.com is a great resource. It tells us Solomon died in 931 B.C and places our next story, *The Water Girl*, in 863 B.C.—only 68 years later—during the reign of wicked King Ahab and his queen, Jezebel.

Ahab's father, King Omri, brokered the marriage of his son to the Phoenician princess, Jezebel, as a shrewd trade agreement. Phoenicians were, after all, the only supplier and seafaring merchants of the highly sought-after purple dye hoarded by royalty. But Ahab got more than a Phoenician princess and profitable trade. Jezebel also brought her pagan god, **_Baal_**, with all its pleasurable and heinous worship practices. Idolatry swept through Israel like a plague, and when Ahab and Jezebel's daughter married a prince of Judah—the idolatry swept through the southern kingdom, too.

God responded by raising up His greatest prophet, Elijah, who stood like a beacon on Mt. Carmel. He challenged the priests of Baal to an ancient-style duel—god vs. God. After three years of drought, Elijah called for someone to douse the altar with water (1 Kings 18:33).

Who do you suppose found a water source—and then carried jug-after-jug all the way up Mt. Carmel? Perhaps it was...*The Water Girl.*

One

> *"[Ahab] took for his wife Jezebel the daughter of Ethbaal king of the Sidonians, and went and served Baal and worshiped him. He erected an altar for Baal ... And Ahab made an Asherah. Ahab did more to provoke the Lord, the God of Israel, to anger than all the kings of Israel who were before him."*
> **1 Kings 16:31-33**

Miriam

The cloying smells of incense, blood, and sweat swirled around me in the lamp-lit sanctuary of Baal's temple. Making my way to the altar with a half-full bucket of water, I was cautious not to spill a drop.

"Water Girl!" the high priest snarled, waving for me to hurry. I tried, but the sticky floor grabbed at my bare feet.

It had been weeks since I'd cleaned it, but I dared not waste precious water on the mundane task. I'd been whipped for less. Carefully, I placed the bucket beside the priest, bowed, and turned to go.

"Wait." He grabbed my arm, his bloody hand like a vice. "Bring another bucket. There's a line of worshipers out the door." I grudgingly glanced up, and he directed me with a nod. I should have kept my head bowed. Only hungry eyes met mine, and I immediately thought of my older sister, Rachel, as lovely as the matriarch for whom she was named. Which of these men's "offerings" would she be forced to receive in Asherah's tent after the priest divined their future? I ached for her and felt traitorous relief that I'd been blessed with the face of a dog.

Perhaps the high priest could help. "My sister is very strong," I whispered. "She could help me carry buckets."

"Your sister is more valuable as a priestess. Now, get my water." He shoved me toward the kitchen.

I hurried toward the door behind the altar. When I looked back, he'd already used half the water to wash only one sheep's entrails. Why couldn't he read bloody entrails? Furious at his careless waste, my life, the gods, and the Yahweh prophet who pronounced this wretched drought three years ago, I banged the kitchen door open.

Elika, the cook, clucked her tongue. "You'll surely get a beating before the day ends with that attitude." She was as sassy as I, but old enough to get away with it.

"How am I supposed to provide water when the high priest uses it as if it's common as air?" I swiped at tears, betrayed by my own emotions. I was too old to be a child and too young to be a woman. My sister said my heart was a warrior's, and I should have been a man.

"Water Gi—" The priest's summons was drowned out by royal trumpets.

Elika rolled her eyes. "A second visit from Queen Jezebel today? Will they ever go back to their palace in Samaria?" She rubbed wheat kernels between her palms harder than usual and puffed away the chaff. "Jezreel is full of simple people—more like hardy chickens, not fancy enough for the king's peacock." She flapped her elbows and crowed, almost making me forget my sour mood—and the water I'd been sent to fetch.

"Water! Girl!" Anger punctuated the priest's summons, flinging both Elika and me into action.

"Take my pitcher. I'll go to the well and have your bucket ready when you return."

"Thank you." I kissed the old woman's wrinkle-soft cheek before hurrying away. But the door barely opened. I shoved my shoulder against it harder, and two bald-headed priests peered around, opening enough for me and the pitcher to slip through. The line of worshipers had been replaced by white-robed, Baal priests—and Queen Jezebel. Packed full, the temple sanctuary was like a solid wheel with the high priest and queen in the center beside the altar.

"Water Girl!" the priest shouted again.

"Here!" I squeaked. Priests pushed my rail-thin frame through the tightly-packed mass of bodies while I guarded the pitcher against my chest. Finally, emerging into the clearing around the altar, I could do nothing but stare at the royal peacock. Her eyes glowed with green malachite powder around them, and her lips were as red as fresh blood. Her robes bore every color of the rainbow, generously woven with gold thread and gems that sparkled with the altar's fire.

Snatching the pitcher from me, the priest seethed, "Did you go all the way to a mountain spring to fetch it?"

I gave no reply, too mesmerized by the queen's stare. Her black eyes had no color to soften her gaze. They'd locked onto mine, boring into my soul, intent on destroying whatever life I had left.

A terrifying grin curved her lips. "You still follow Yahweh," she whispered.

"No, my queen!" I said too quickly, heart racing. "My family renounced the God of our fathers years ago. We have not followed the laws of our people since I was a child." And I'd told no one how I wished the old stories of Yahweh were true. Not since Jezebel had killed all Yahweh's prophets and threatened to exterminate others in the land who dared confess allegiance to Him.

Her eyes narrowed with a last glare before turning to face the room packed with priests. My shoulders sagged with relief until I heard the sharp edge in her voice. "Elijah has finally crawled out from under the rock where he's been hiding and challenged my priests to a contest. Every one of you, as well as the priests in Asherah's service, will appear on Mount Carmel the dawn after tomorrow to prove once and for all that our gods are greater than the Hebrews' archaic deity."

She turned back to the high priest and said, "King Ahab has sent messengers throughout Israel to summon all the people to this contest. Baal will not fail us." She leaned close, lowering her voice. "You will show Elijah Baal's power and then Elijah will become our sacrifice."

"Yes, my queen." He bowed, remaining bent—no doubt to avoid meeting her terrifying gaze.

She looked at me instead. "You, little water girl, will know for certain which gods to trust when Baal and Asherah unleash their power on Mt. Carmel."

Two

> "When Ahab saw Elijah, Ahab said to him, 'Is it you, you troubler of Israel?' And he answered, 'I have not troubled Israel, but you have, and your father's house, because you have abandoned the commandments of the Lord and followed the Baals. Now therefore send and gather all Israel to me at Mount Carmel, and the 450 prophets of Baal and the 400 prophets of Asherah, who eat at Jezebel's table.'"
> **1 Kings 18:17-19**

I laid on my sleeping mat after an exhausting day of packing and travel, listening to the other servants' deep and steady breathing. Where was Rachel? The priestesses had been required to receive offerings up until the moment we left Jezreel, but I'd seen her in the caravan and told her which tent would be ours at the foot of Mt. Carmel. Three other priestesses had already finished their duties, washed their faces, and fallen onto their mats in an exhausted slumber.

Jezebel's announcement of the gods' contest had stirred frenzied activity among the priests and temple servants but also excitement among the people of Jezreel. All those who had waited to give their offerings followed the extensive caravan on our full day's walk to Mt. Carmel, where Elijah's contest would take place. While the servants set up camp at the foot of the mountain, the priests and priestesses began the arduous labor of sacrifices and offerings atop the mount, staying late into the night.

There was little demand for divining, but so many worshipers wished to give offerings under the stars that I was sent to the priestess's quarters to help dress—and re-dress—the young women for service. After each *offering* they received, each girl was anointed with oil by Asherah's high priestess. Makeup refreshed, scanty robes changed if necessary, and then they were sent back to the line of priestesses awaiting the next offering.

I'd never personally witnessed my sister Rachel's circuit of humiliation until tonight. Though she was two years older than me, she'd served here only two weeks. I'd served in Baal's temple a year. I was too ugly to marry, but Abba thought surely he could find Rachel a husband. I'd seen the life slowly drain from my sister's eyes as she withdrew into herself more each day. This drought had ruined more than our fields.

The tent flap fluttered, and I rose up on one elbow. Moonlight spilled in, showing Rachel's silhouette.

"Over here," I croaked in a whisper. She scanned the patchwork of sleeping forms, found me, and nodded. Holding a single oil lamp aloft, she stepped over the other eighteen servants and priestesses who shared our tent, careful not to wake them.

I'd unrolled her mat beside me and now patted it. "Why are you so much later than the others?" I asked as she folded her legs and sat. But when the lamplight drew nearer her face, all other questions ceased. "Who beat you?"

Her swollen lips pursed together as water filled her eyes. Shaking violently, tears spilled down her cheeks, but her lips remained tightly shut—words locked behind emotions racing across her beautiful but battered face.

I took the lamp from her hand, placed it on the ground

beside us, and drew her into my arms. She winced. I retrieved the lamp to peer under her rough spun robe. Fresh bruises. Tears burned my eyes as I pulled her into a gentler embrace and rocked her the way Ima had done when we were children. Then I began singing one of David's psalms.

"Shut up, girl!" One of the women hissed. "Do you want to get us all killed?"

I quieted my song to just a whisper against Rachel's ear. "Even though I walk through the valley of the shadow of death, I will fear no evil—"

She pulled away, eyes downcast. "You haven't seen this kind of evil, Miriam." Her words came on a sob. Shaking her head, she kept her voice low. "I can't do it. I can't live like this. I'd rather die."

"I know, but you can't. We'll think of something." I sounded so brave, but what could two girls do in a country ravaged by drought? If we fled to the trade routes, our fate would be the same—only without a priest or priestess to feed us.

She suddenly pulled me close, pressing a whisper against my hair. "The king has summoned all of Israel to the contest tomorrow. We can escape into the crowd."

"But I must carry water for the high priest and—"

"Miriam," she said, shaking me, "it's our only chance!"

I gently pulled away and brushed her bruised cheek, aching for the deeper pain I saw in her wild eyes. "All right, my sister. We'll find a way."

Three

[King Ahab said to Obadiah,] "Go through the land to all the springs of water and to all the valleys. Perhaps we may find grass and save the horses and mules alive, and not lose some of the animals."
1 Kings 18:5

Rachel and I had barely finished coating her wounds with honey and winding a tight bandage around her ribs when Asherah's high priestess sounded the bells, calling all priestesses to prepare the small tents around the altar on Mt. Carmel. Jezebel had ordered every priestess to wear makeup like the queen's own so that when the Israelites brought offerings after the gods' victory, they'd feel as if they celebrated with the queen herself.

"I can't go back," Rachel's hands were sweaty, eyes wide with panic. "What if the same man who beat me last night comes into my tent again?"

"We'll get out before the offerings begin," I promised Rachel, tearing my hand from her grasp. "If Baal and Asherah win, meet me at the spring here in camp."

"But If—"

"Go, Rachel. I'll see you at the contest." She released my hand, but as I watched her walk away, despair filled me. I was one of twenty girls who would carry water for 450 Baal priests, and Rachel was one of a hundred priestesses receiving offerings after the 400 Asherah priests interceded for worshipers. How could either of us step away from our duties long enough to find a willing soul to sneak us away from the celebration that would follow? Who would be foolish enough to cross swords with Jezebel's beloved priests by helping a servant girl and a priestess escape?

While the other women and girls in our tent rolled their sleeping mats, splashed their faces with water, and dressed for the day, I sat in yesterday's clothes and entertained an even more traitorous thought.

Yahweh, if I dared pray to You for rescue, would You help us?

I watched the women bustling around my chamber as if they might have heard my silent plea. Of course, they were oblivious, so I ventured more conversation with the God of my fathers. *Yahweh, if You're there, Rachel and I need You today. We are daughters of Manasseh's tribe—the son of the patriarch Joseph, who was treacherously sold by his brothers into Egypt. But You used Joseph's hardship to bring about good for all Israel's sons when a drought threatened this same land. Can You . . . would You . . . bring about good from hardship once again? Not because I am great like our father Joseph, but because I want to believe You are real.*

I waited for a sign. Some sort of flicker of my lamp's flame or a whisper amid the noise in the tent. But no sign came. I heard only the grumbling of exhausted servants.

"Hurry up, Miriam." A water girl named Tirzah lodged a fist against one hip. "Why should others carry a greater burden because you move slower than honey in winter?"

Jumping to my feet, I stood a hand-breadth taller and leaned close. "You're just jealous I was chosen to serve the high priest. Maybe you and the other girls should work more and talk less."

A sly smile curved her lips. "You were chosen for the high priest's service because you're too ugly to *ever* be a priestess. At least the other girls and I will one day wear veils and lovely robes and serve in Asherah's tents."

"Oh, Tirzah, no!" Shocked, my animosity fled and I reached for her hand. "It's not exciting like you think."

She pulled away and stepped back. "I see your sister bringing you venison and lamb from the Queen's table while we eat bread and stew day-after-day. I'm tired of it," she said, her voice warbling. Clearing her throat, she rolled back her shoulders. "So put away your mat, Miriam, and report to the high priest. If we can prove Yahweh's prophet powerless and gain Baal's favor, perhaps then, he'll bring rain to Israel again."

I watched her walk away, feeling pity for her. Not only was she deluded about the life of a priestess, she was silly to think that *any* god could make it rain in the middle of an Israel summer. Baal had descended to the Netherworld three years ago, and he'd never returned to couple with Asherah and fertilize the earth—no matter how many times the Israelites brought their offerings. I'd heard rumors that it was Elijah's word from Yahweh that closed the heavens three years ago, but to admit such a thing would be to admit Yahweh's power over Jezebel's gods—and such an admission was certain death.

Tirzah was right about one thing. I needed to roll up my mat and report to the high priest, or I'd be punished severely. After quickly completing my tasks, I grabbed a piece of bread and hard cheese from the servants' basket and hurried out of the tent. The other girls were already at the mountain spring, but they stood idle, buckets overturned at their feet.

"What is it?" I asked, joining them.

"It's dry," Tirzah spat. "There's only a mud puddle. No water. What do we do now?"

I groaned inwardly. *Yahweh, this isn't a very promising start for a rescue.* "We must tell the high priest."

Tirzah choked on a laugh. "*You* must tell him, Miriam, since you're his servant." She glanced at the other girls before adding, "I wouldn't want to be the one to disappoint the high priest *or* the queen today."

Four

"Obadiah ... was over the household. (Now Obadiah feared the Lord greatly, and when Jezebel cut off the prophets of the Lord, Obadiah took a hundred prophets and hid them by fifties in a cave and fed them with bread and water.)"
1 Kings 18:3-4

"There's barely a trickle of water from the spring at the base of the mountain," I explained.

The high priest's jaw went slack, his eyes wide. "*You* will tell the queen what you saw." He grabbed my ear and dragged me toward the royal dais where King Ahab, Queen Jezebel, and a few royal counselors were already seated and watching the preparations.

The high priest unceremoniously flung me to the ground before them. "Tell your queen what you told me."

I dared not look at her. "The spring at the base of Mt. Carmel is dry, my queen."

The high priest added, "Your priests cannot divine the gods' messages from bloody entrails."

I ventured a momentary glance at Jezebel. She glared at me while tapping a henna-stained fingernail against her red lips.

"Water Girl, you are an especially troublesome creature, and this is twice now that I've had to look at you. I fear I might have to kill you if you don't find water for my priests. What good is a *water girl* if she can't carry water?"

Having no doubt she'd make good her threat, I had no reason to be cautious with my words. I was dead anyway. Still kneeling, I straightened my back and squared my shoulders but kept my eyes averted. "Didn't we come to Mt. Carmel to prove Baal and Asherah superior to Yahweh, my queen? Why would we dim the brilliant display of our gods with petty, individual divinations?"

Jezebel scooted to the edge of her throne and I glimpsed her wry grin, so I ventured more in hopes of salvation. "Why not demand every eye focused on your valiant priests as they call upon the gods who will certainly break the back of Elijah's threats today?" With no water to carry and every eye focused on her priests, perhaps I could slip unnoticed through the audience and find someone willing to secret Rachel and me away from this place.

Jezebel threw her head back and cackled—enough to gain the attention of nearly everyone on Mt. Carmel. My cheeks burned at the spectacle, and even King Ahab placed a hand on her arm to quiet her. "The girl is amusing, my dear," he said, "but what is your decision? They're your priests, so I leave today's details to you."

Fanning herself as if she'd run a race, she ignored me and spoke to her high priest. "There will be no divining today and no individual offerings taken for Asherah. The priests will focus their full attention on Israel's well-being."

The high priest bowed. "It will be as you command, my queen."

When he grabbed my arm to drag me away, the queen shouted, "Wait." We both turned slowly and found her smiling like an Egyptian cat watching a mouse. "The girl amuses me." She looked over the king's right shoulder to a gray-haired man dressed in fine clothes with a kind face. "Obadiah, she is to serve me on the dais."

The man inclined his head in a slight bow. "As you command, my queen." He offered his hand and then smiled at me—like my abba used to do when I was a little girl.

My breath caught and I felt a sudden urge to run into his arms. The thought was fleeting, however, when the high priest's hand clamped hard on my shoulder. "But, my queen, Water Girl is very useful to the priests, and her sister has only begun her training as a priestess. I fear separating them—"

"Is your sister as outspoken as you are?" The queen interrupted, spearing me with her eyes.

"She can be if you like," I said.

Chuckling, she nodded at Obadiah. "Go find her sister as well. They can both serve us during today's contest."

Obadiah hurried off the dais, removed the priest's hand from my shoulder, and then placed himself between us. "Where is her sister?"

The priest sneered. "I'm not a keeper of Asherah's priestesses."

"Neither are you this girl's keeper anymore." Taking my hand, he led me away like a victor after battle.

I covered a giggle and whispered, "If I ever have to go back to the temple, I'll get such a beating." I sobered quickly, remembering my promise of escape with Rachel.

"What?" Obadiah stopped and looked down at me, his brow lined with concern. "You need not worry. I'll do everything in my power to ensure you and your sister *never* return to temple service." He leaned in, smiling conspiratorially. "And as the king's palace administrator, it is well within my power to do so."

Was this the rescue Yahweh had provided? I didn't want to be *closer* to the wicked queen. I wanted to be away from her and from Jezreel! But we would never find someone to sneak us away if we served on the dais all day. And how could I confess such a thing to the third most powerful man in Israel? I couldn't—not even to a man whose brown eyes were as warm as my ima's fresh bread.

"Thank you, my lord," I said instead, bowing my head to hide the disappointment. "I'm sure Rachel will also be grateful."

Five

"Elijah came near to all the people and said, 'How long will you go limping between two different opinions? If the Lord is God, follow him; but if Baal, then follow him.' And the people did not answer him a word."
1 Kings 18:21

When Obadiah and I found Rachel and returned to the dais to serve the queen, she saw my sister's beaten face and decided Rachel wouldn't provide the right *image* for today's celebration. She'd commanded that I be dressed in a blue-linen robe, and somehow, Obadiah's whispered conversation with King Ahab made it possible for Rachel to stay with us on the dais—if she remained hidden. Perhaps this palace administrator was a part of Yahweh's answer to my prayer after all.

Obadiah stood at the king's right shoulder, and I stood beside Queen Jezebel. Huddled behind the king's make-shift throne, Rachel reached up to tug on my sleeve. "I need something to drink," she whispered, dry mouth crackling.

We hadn't drunk anything since dawn. Elijah arrived soon after in his dirty, rough-spun, brown robe, shaggy hair and unkempt beard. With his challenge, everyone believed we'd see a great spectacle of the gods' power and be feasting by midday. But the sun was nearly overhead now, and the Israelites—gathered as far as the eye could see—were becoming restless in the unrelenting heat while Jezebel's priests and priestesses continued their chanting and pleading.

I leaned down to whisper, "I know it's hot, Rachel, but when the gods answer, we'll be able to leave the dais and find something to drink—somewhere." My eyes lingered on her, hoping to communicate I hadn't given up on our escape plan. When I resumed my pose beside the queen, I caught a glimpse of Obadiah, deep concern lining his brow. He looked at Rachel, then again at me, and then pulled a waterskin from his belt. He handed it to my sister, and she drank like a desert wanderer.

I mouthed the words, *thank you,* to the man who had saved us more than once today. Why was he helping? And how had someone so kind survived in Ahab's royal household?

This morning, Obadiah had stood silently at the king's side when the prophet Elijah marched confidently to Carmel's mount and levied his challenge. "How long will you waver between two opinions?" Elijah shouted at the people of Israel, his voice carrying in every direction. "If the Lord is God, follow him; but if Baal, then follow him."

His words pierced my own soul. I'd been wrestling with my allegiance to gods all my life, but how could I decide when I saw no evidence of their power?

"I'm the only one of Yahweh's prophets left," Elijah had said, "but there are 450 of Baal's priests who eat at Jezebel's table. We'll use two bulls in a contest. The priests of Baal should go first, cutting their bull into pieces." He turned to the 450 priests. "Arrange the pieces on your altar, and let your god set fire to it. After that, I'll cut up my sacrifice and ask Yahweh to do the same."

Had something familiar passed between Obadiah and Yahweh's prophet while Baal's priests slaughtered their bull?

After arranging the pieces of meat on the altar, the priests recited a few chants and incantations, and expectation hummed in the silence. Surely Baal, the storm god, could easily ignite the sacrifice with a bolt of lightning. But no fire. And the sun—now overhead—beat down mercilessly. The priests had resumed their chanting, their incantations, and had even resorted to dancing.

"More wine!" Jezebel screeched over the priests' noise. I hurried to fill her gold goblet, and she waved me away. Her eyes were locked on the altar so intently, I thought her stare might ignite it if the gods did not.

"Maybe you should yell louder!" Elijah's nasally shout sliced through the droning. "Or perhaps Baal is sleeping or relieving himself."

Jezebel bolted to her feet. "Kill him!"

But the king shouted, "No! We will finish the contest and let the gods speak for themselves." He waved off the royal guard and glared at Yahweh's prophet.

Baal's high priest approached the altar, lifted his arms and cried out, "Oh mighty Baal! Answer our pleas!" Taking his dagger from its sheath, he drew the blade across his hand. A priestess appeared with a bowl, and the priest squeezed his fist over it, draining his own blood to capture the god's attention. The priestess lifted the bowl to her lips and drank, then shared it with others as the chanting continued. Other priests repeated the high priest's sacrifice, offering their blood too, while the priestesses danced in a frenzy.

Still, no fire fell, and only flies showed interest in the meat on their altar.

The sun continued its snail's pace across the cloudless sky, and I grew faint. Behind the thrones, Obadiah handed me his goblet of watered wine and silently encouraged me to drink. I was too weary and weak to fear the consequences if I was discovered, but I still hid behind the queen's throne as I drained the goblet dry. He poured more from the royal supplies and offered it to Rachel. Our savior again.

Even some of the priests had been taken back to camp, unconscious from loss of blood and dehydration. Those who continued their relentless incantations seemed to move as a dream. Slowly, each motion labored; their voices raspy and weak.

Elijah approached the dais in his worn sandals, a wide grin on his craggy face. "It would appear your gods have gone on some sort of holiday."

Jezebel's growl was indescribably feral. King Ahab spoke before she could respond. "Begin your sacrifice, prophet."

As Elijah walked through the crowd of priests, the queen threw her gold goblet at him but missed. "Aahh!" She cried in frustration, panting with fury.

I looked to Obadiah, who nodded in the direction of the goblet, silently ordering me to fetch it. Happy to get away from Jezebel and her tantrum, I rushed off the dais, dodging bloody priests and dancing priestesses.

When I did, I ran headlong into the wild-haired Yahweh prophet, who had stopped a short distance away.

As I bent to pick up the queen's goblet, he hefted a large rock beside it and whispered, "Will you continue to waver between two opinions, little Miriam?" Then he walked quickly away, gathering more rocks to rebuild an old altar.

I stood like a statue, holding the goblet and staring after him. *Little Miriam.* How did he know my name? Had he really spoken to me, or had I imagined it? *Will you continue to waver between two opinions?*

"Water Girl!" The queen shouted. "Get back here!"

I rushed to the dais, but before I could wipe her goblet with a clean cloth, she grabbed my wrist. "What did the maniac say to you?"

Glancing first at Obadiah, I hoped for some direction on

how to reply—the truth or a lie. He offered an almost indiscernible shake of his head, and I took the warning.

"He offered to pick up your goblet for me. I refused."

"You should have kicked him in the teeth," Jezebel said, releasing my wrist. "But you were right not to let him touch you or my goblet." She settled back on her throne and watched the prophet assemble his altar. "Get me more wine, so I can enjoy Elijah's final attempt to stay alive."

I did as she asked and then also turned to watch Yahweh's prophet systematically rebuild an altar that Israelites had destroyed years ago. Even Jezebel's priests had finally stopped their frenzied begging and sat quietly beside their own altar. Elijah, having called people from the crowd to gather around him, spoke loudly as he worked. "I'm using twelve large stones," he explained, "according to the number of the tribes of the sons of Jacob, to whom the Lord said, 'Israel will be your name.'"

When he began digging a trench around his new altar, murmurs of speculation fluttered over the gathering. Why a trench? The bull's blood would soak into the parched earth.

His strange activity drew the mocking of Baal's priests. "Will that ditch catch your tears when your god doesn't answer?" Jezebel laughed loud and long, one hand gripping her goblet so tightly, her knuckles were white.

The prophet ignored their jibes, retrieving the pieces of wood from his mule and placing them carefully on the altar. His lips moved, but the boasting and mocking was replaced with silent reverence. Elijah then approached the bull that had been tethered all day. Six men with ropes held it steady while Elijah placed one arm over its neck, whispered in its ear, and slit its throat. Then the men held the ropes taut until the bull dropped.

What had the prophet whispered to the beast moments before he took its life? Was Elijah mad? An indescribable emotion gripped my chest. Darker than disappointment.

Sadder than anger. I hadn't realized how much I wanted Yahweh's prophet to win this contest.

The man divided his sacrifice adeptly, restoring a tiny measure of my hope. When he finished placing each piece on the altar, he turned to the dais and locked his eyes on me. "Water Girl," he shouted. "Gather the others to help you fill four jars with water and pour it on the offering."

Queen Jezebel rose slowly from her throne and turned a murderous look on me. "Go to the spring," she said. "The same one you checked this morning."

My legs felt wooden, reluctant to move. The other girls appeared at the front of the crowd, waiting for me to descend the dais. I swallowed hard, caught between two worlds. The queen's lethal glare followed me down the steps, but Elijah grinned while offering Tirzah, me, and two others girls four clay pitchers. My thoughts raced faster than my feet. If we found water at the spring, there could be no doubt which God wielded the greater power.

Six

"And when all the people saw it, they fell on their faces and said, *The Lord, he is God; the Lord, he is God.*"
1 Kings 18:39

"This is ridiculous," Tirzah whispered as we shouldered our way through the crowd. "The spring is dry. Why didn't you simply tell the old fool there isn't any water?"

I stopped abruptly, and the three girls stumbled into me. But I pulled them into a tight circle to share something only with them. "We have to try. What if Elijah's God is real? What if Yahweh wants to prove His power today? What if, like Elijah said, we must make a choice about which God to serve?"

"Don't talk like that!" Tirzah looked around us and shoved me forward. "I'll follow you to the spring," she said in a coarse whisper, "but I won't die for you."

We continued in silence, dodging people everywhere. The soldiers guarding our camp let us pass, and I led the others to the spring that had always flowed with fresh mountain water—until this morning. When we were twenty paces away, I heard water splashing.

"Yahweh is real." The words passed over my lips in a whisper as my feet carried me to the proof. There, flowing down from an outcropping of rocks, water came crashing down with a force equal to a wadi's flood after winter rains. All four of us stood in reverent silence, water jars still perched on our heads, watching the undeniable glory of our fathers' God.

Finally, I chuckled and swung the jar to the ground. "We'd better hurry and get the water to Elijah so the rest of Israel can know what we know." Two of the girls began filling their jars, and after a moment's hesitation, Tirzah joined us. When Elijah ordered a second round—and a third—poured onto the altar, our troop of girls anxiously obeyed.

Elijah poured all twelve jars on the sacrifice and handed them to me empty as he finished. We were both drenched but exchanged a happy, knowing grin that the trench around Yahweh's altar was now full-to-overflowing.

The prophet turned his face skyward, and I looked up expectantly as he prayed. "O Lord, God of Abraham, Isaac, and Israel, let it be known this day that You are the only *true* God in Israel, and that I have done all these things at Your command. Answer me, Yahweh, so that these people will know that You alone are God, and that You have turned their hearts back."

Before the last word died on his lips, a pillar of fire fell from the sky. I screamed, covering my head and falling to my knees, the heat of the blaze more intense than any fire of this world—yet it didn't burn me. I felt a hand tugging at my arm, pulling me to my feet. When I stood, Elijah tugged me close, and we watched together as Yahweh's presence consumed the sacrifice, the wood, the stones, and even licked up the water from the trench.

The crowd all around us—on top of Mt. Carmel and on every slope and valley—had fallen on their faces and were shouting, "El-i-Jah! El-i-Jah! God is Yahweh! God is Yahweh!" Shouting Elijah's name, with the fullness of its meaning moving from their lips to their hearts through the power of Yahweh's mighty hand. The people of Israel no longer wavered in their opinion between the vague gods of Canaan with their catch-all title *El*. No. Yahweh wasn't one of many. The only *El* was Yahweh.

As I scanned the Jezreel Valley below us, a rainbow-colored robe fluttered from a racing chariot with a single driver. The queen hadn't bowed, but at least she hadn't ordered the mass extermination of our nation.

Elijah pointed to the chariot. "Israel will never be safe as long as that woman sits beside Ahab on her throne, but the faithful must be willing to stand strong, Little Miriam." He released me and with uplifted hands, quieted the crowd. Standing only ten paces from Jezebel's priests, he waited until the whole earth seemed utterly silent and then shouted, "Seize the priests and let none escape!"

Horrified, I ran to the dais to find Rachel as the whole gathering overpowered the weak and bloodied priests. I pulled Rachel into my arms, and she buried her face against my shoulder.

"Get back to the palace," the king said to Obadiah. "Tell the queen I'll come as soon as I've contained Yahweh's prophet."

"Yes, my king." The moment Ahab stepped off the dais, Obadiah pulled us into his arms.

I peeked over Rachel's shoulder and saw Elijah leading the mob off the mountain. "We'll slaughter the priests at the brook of Kidron." A victory cry rose from the mob and sent a shiver down my spine.

Then—a strange hush descended. The king had followed the mob, his royal guards with him. Only Obadiah remained with us. "Girls, listen to me," he said, coaxing us to look him. "I believe Yahweh has given you to me to protect. Elijah was wrong. He's not the only Yahweh prophet left. I've hidden a hundred others from Jezebel's murderous threats and have been feeding them for three years. They're in need of women to help them cook and do simple tasks like mending and washing. He paused, seeming to measure Rachel's reaction and then searched my face. "They might even teach you to read and write if you're interested. Though if you'd rather come to the palace with me, I can always assign—"

I threw my arms around his neck, tears clogging my throat. "You are Yahweh's answer to my prayer, Lord Obadiah. We would love to serve the prophets and stay as far away from Jezebel and her priests as possible."

Rachel's arms came around mine, doubling our thanks to this kind and generous man. "I never knew my sister prayed to Yahweh like me, but I'm so grateful that neither of us waver between two opinions any longer."

Author's Note

While researching this story, I discovered there really was a spring at the base of Mt. Carmel! And there's been much discussion over the centuries about how they could have produced approximately twelve gallons of water to drench Elijah's altar and sacrifice. That's an easy answer: GOD! If He could lap it up with fire from heaven, why couldn't he produce the water to douse the altar? So writing a story about the one who discovered the restored water supply was a fun place to start on this little story.

Wells can run dry in a drought, but *springs* seldom do. Here's a more "official" description of the difference:

A well is a hole bored in the ground you can pump water out of. A spring is where <u>natural</u> hydraulic forces cause water to bubble up right out of the ground. (https://www.quora.com/Whats-the-difference-between-well-and-spring-water)

I often say the Holy Spirit is a *spring* of Living Water in us, not a *well* because He bubbles up in us. He's the Source, not us. He provides unquenchable power, wisdom, understanding—and anything else He knows we need.

If we feel dry, why is that? Ephesians 4:30 and 1 Thessalonians 5:19 tell us we can quench (or grieve) the Spirit. During

Ahab's reign, the people of Israel "wavered between two opinions," and Elijah challenged them to choose. Have you committed your heart, soul, mind, and strength to the one, true God?

> *"I know your deeds, that you are neither cold nor hot.*
> *I wish you were either one or the other!"*
> **Revelation 3:15**

Ask Jesus to show Himself to you today, and then watch for His presence to be revealed. He is real. He is alive. The LORD, He is God—and He is a Spring of Living Water that never runs dry!

The Mole's Wife

Note to Reader

Occasionally, I write short stories that expand on characters or events found in my novels. Though the main characters in *The Mole's Wife* are fictional, the story itself expands on biblical events and characters during King Hezekiah's reign (2 Kings 18-20; 2 Chronicles 29-32). I write about Hezekiah's tumultuous childhood and courtship with his eventual queen, Hephzibah, in my novel, *Isaiah's Daughter*. But don't worry! You won't find any spoilers in *The Mole's Wife* that would ruin *Isaiah's Daughter* if you choose to read it later. And you need not have read *Isaiah's Daughter* to understand what you're about to read in this short story.

So why read *The Mole's Wife*?

There's a particular element in *Isaiah's Daughter* that has only a fleeting mention in Scripture but has perplexed historians and archaeologists for centuries:

> *"As for the other events of Hezekiah's reign, all his achievements and* **how he made the pool and the tunnel by which he brought water into the city,** *are they not written in the book of the annals of the kings of Judah?"*
> **2 Kings 20:20 (*emphasis* added)**

I've been fascinated by Hezekiah's Tunnel since 2000. Someone described it to me only weeks after we returned from Israel. That's right—only weeks *after* our first tour of Israel, I discovering we'd *missed seeing this tunnel!* I must confess to breaking the tenth commandment and vehemently envied my neighbor's Israel tour.

So I studied the tunnel. Watched YouTube videos about it. I even included information about the tunnel in three of my novels. We made sure to include a tour of Hezekiah's Tunnel on our March 2020 Tour of Israel itinerary, and then—COVID-19 exploded *while* we were in Israel. Though we toured almost everything on our itinerary with little disruption (thankfully), the ministry of tourism shut down ALL touring the night before our last day in Jerusalem. The night before we were scheduled to see Hezekiah's Tunnel and the City of David. After a serious, boo-hoo-hiccup cry, I accepted the circumstance as my God's promise that I'd return to Israel again someday to see those very important sites!

Hezekiah's Tunnel still looms large in my imagination, and I often ponder the men responsible for its construction. Nothing like it had ever been done before. Never even attempted! They weren't just digging a few feet below the surface of soft soil. These skilled engineers used pickaxes and hammers, ingenuity that we can't even fathom, and pounded their way deep through a granite mountain. They started on opposite sides and—only by God's intervention—they connected their blind digging somewhere deep inside the earth.

Dangerous? You bet. So...I wondered about their wives. How did these brave women feel, waiting nervously at home while praying for their husbands' safety? I hope as you read *The Mole's Wife*, you'll feel both fear and wonder as the city of Jerusalem awaits Assyria's certain attack—the most ruthless army the world had ever known.

ONE

*"In the fourteenth year of King Hezekiah, Sennacherib king of
Assyria came up against
all the fortified cities of Judah and took them."*
2 Kings 18:13

JERUSHA

My husband had gained his high standing from the lowest occupation in Jerusalem. Known as Judah's Mole, Daniel had spent most of his life digging wells, patching cisterns, and diagraming and maintaining mines and quarries. He felt most at home underground, and he was paid handsomely for it. But no amount of silver could compensate for the terror on his features now.

"I had to get away from the digging, but I can't stay long." He pulled me into trembling arms. "It's insanity, Jerusha. No one has ever started a tunnel from both sides of a mountain and connected in the middle. King Hezekiah doesn't understa—"

"The Assyrians are coming." I squeezed him, halting his rant. "The king understands *that*, Daniel."

He stilled and looked down at me, hopelessness painting dark circles around his eyes.

I'd never seen him so haunted, but I couldn't let him see my concern. "You need a little time to rest, and you'll be fine." I led him to a cushion beside my work table, tugged at him to sit, and began kneading his shoulders. Tomorrow's bread dough could wait.

He swiped both hands down his face and let his head fall forward. "I know the Assyrians are coming, Jerusha, but urgency can't change human limitations. Eliakim and I have studied Mount Zion's fissures for ten years, but there's no guarantee we'll ever connect the Gihon Spring outside the city's wall to the Upper Pool inside the gates." He shrugged me away and slammed his hand on the table, leveraging himself to stand so he could glare down at me again. "Why must *everyone* push me beyond reason?" Sweat beaded on his brow; his nostrils flared. I'd known Daniel ben Josiah since I was a little girl. He was afraid, not angry.

Feigning courage, I sniffed back tears and lifted my chin. "I'm not pushing, but I'll remind you that Yahweh works best when urgency drives us past human limitations." I sounded brave, but this morning's market gossip ran chariot races in my mind. Assyrian troops were expected to attack Judah's northern villages in three days. Panic had spread so quickly, King Hezekiah closed Jerusalem's gates at midday. Swiping at stubborn tears, I glimpsed my hand and realized it was I who trembled, not my husband.

"Jerusha, I'm sorry." My gentle giant wrapped me in a cocoon of his strength and pulled me onto his cushion, holding me like a child. "My first visit home in six days and I flog you with harsh words. Can you forgive me, my love?"

I clung to him and prayed, *Yahweh, how can I tell him my news when he's in such a state?* "Of course, I forgive you, but you must not lose hope, Daniel. Remember, you're not alone in the depths of the earth."

"I know. Eliakim is a genius. Without his engineering skills, we wouldn't have gotten this far."

"That's not who I meant."

"Of course, the forced-labor has worked beyond human endurance." He sighed, resting his chin atop my head. "We've all worked day and night, resting only to eat when our families bring—"

I broke free of him and pressed a hand over his mouth. "Yahweh. *Yahweh* is helping you."

He kissed my palm and forced a smile. "Of course," he said but then closed his eyes in a lingering hush.

I leaned back against his chest, hoping he'd share his thoughts. After ten years of marriage, I should have known better. "Is it the dig that silenced you? Or something else?"

An extended pause, and finally he sighed before answering. "I haven't considered Yahweh in weeks." He fell silent again, and I knew not to press him. He needed my presence, not prodding, so I laced my fingers with his and waited. "What if I ask Yahweh to intervene—and then I fail?" he whispered. "Does that mean God refused to rescue His people? Or—" Another hesitation. "Does it mean Yahweh isn't real?"

The honesty sounded almost blasphemous, but how many times had I felt the same about my barrenness? In all our years of marriage, not once had I conceived. And I'd stopped praying for a baby years ago. Yahweh's silence was too painful.

A chill ran through me, so I pulled his arms around me like a blanket. "Yahweh *is* with us," I said, as much to reassure myself as Daniel. Then I did something I'd never done before. "Please, Yahweh," I prayed, "give all the men working on the tunnel wisdom, strength, and stamina to connect the spring and bring water into our city so we can withstand a siege."

Daniel nudged me aside and faced me. "Your prayer presupposes Assyria's siege, Jerusha. Will God let us rot inside these walls for three years like Israel did in Samaria?" His words dripped with bitterness, and I wanted to defend Yahweh—but could I?

What if Assyria conquered and scattered Jerusalem to foreign lands as they'd done to Israel's northern tribes? Pressing a hand against my belly, I felt a wave of nausea, considering the hardships my child might endure. *Yahweh, we've waited so long. You must have a reason for letting me conceive now.*

I turned to face him, and he sat a little straighter as if preparing for a blow. "I don't know if the Assyrians will barricade us inside this city," I said, "but I know this, Daniel ben Josiah: Your wife's *and* your child's life depend on connecting those tunnels."

His defenses crumbled with the surprise. "You're . . ." His eyes grew moist as he touched my flat belly as if I might shatter. "Are you sure?"

"The midwife visited today and confirmed it."

"But how?" I lifted my brow, considering he was complicit. He laughed. "I know *how*, but I meant we've tried for so long without success. I'd given up."

"As had I, but Yahweh didn't give up on us." I framed his faced with my hands. "We will keep believing. Keep trusting. Keep asking—and Yahweh will keep answering in His way. In His time." I kissed him and waited until he nodded his agreement.

Though everything in me wanted to fling my arms around him and never let go, *Judah's Mole* was needed elsewhere. "Come." I stood, prodding him. "It's time for my faithful husband to finish building King Hezekiah's tunnel."

He struggled to his feet, groaned, and stretched his hands to the ceiling. I retrieved the shoulder bag he dropped at the doorway and filled it with hard cheese and bread—enough to sustain him for the night. "I'll bring more in the morning."

Grabbing my waist, he turned me to face him and bent—as if to kiss me—but stopped with barely a finger-width between our lips. He grinned. "If Yahweh can give us a baby, He can connect two tunnels inside a mountain."

There was the playful man I married.

I claimed my kiss and gently trapped his lip between my teeth. He chuckled, feigning injury, and I let go. "Maybe we needed a baby," I said as he reached for his bag, "before we could believe Him for a tunnel."

He halted mid-stride but didn't turn. "Hmm." I followed him to the doorway. He turned at the threshold to kiss my forehead. And I watched him walk into the darkness. *Yahweh, fan our flickering hope into faith's burning flame.*

Two

"In that day I will summon my servant, Eliakim son of Hilkiah. . . He will be a father to those who live in Jerusalem and to the people of Judah . . . what he opens no one can shut, and what he shuts no one can open."
Isaiah 22:20-22

Daniel

Tonight's full moon lit Daniel's way, and his worn, leather sandals fell soundlessly as he passed through Upper Jerusalem's cobble-stoned streets into Lower Jerusalem's packed dirt. He'd always felt more comfortable in the Lower City. It's where he and Abba had lived. Where he and Jerusha would live if Eliakim hadn't insisted they be near enough for their wives to support each other while he and Eliakim traveled so much.

Jerusha is pregnant. The thought sent his heart racing. Surely, the pounding of it would wake the whole city. The possibility sobered him, his eyes darting left and right, searching side streets and alleys for people to avoid. Daniel valued his obscurity, and though he was elated by Jerusha's conception, he could count on one hand those with whom he'd share the news. Jerusha's parents would need to know, of course, and Daniel's only friend, Eliakim.

Nearing the southernmost gate of the city, he spotted Eliakim bent over a table, studying the drawing they updated with each day's digging progress. Daniel cupped his hands around his mouth to amplify the distinctive whistle Eliakim would recognize. His friend's head snapped up immediately. Daniel waved, and Eliakim's shoulders seemed to relax.

"We should have connected by now," Eliakim said as he approached. Then, glancing every direction, he leaned close and lowered his voice. "Assyria has attacked villages in Syria and will reach northern Israel tomorrow. They'll strike Judah's northern towns next and could reach Jerusalem within four days."

"Jerusha is with child." Daniel blurted.

Eliakim straightened, eyes looking larger since his cheeks were gaunt. "That's amazing, Daniel." He didn't smile. They'd both heard how Assyrians used their daggers on pregnant women.

"Failing isn't an option." Daniel checked the drawing for changes and found one. "They've come almost a cubit south in the Gihon tunnel." He glanced up at Eliakim but found little encouragement in his friend's response.

"South and west, but who knows if it's enough—or too much."

Daniel sighed and closed his eyes, kneading his forehead. "How do you want me to proceed on the south tunnel? Continue our northeast diagonal or begin a curve?"

A hand landed firmly on his shoulder, and he opened his eyes to Eliakim's intense gaze. "Proceed as Yahweh leads. It appears He's at work in your household, so I trust Him to lead you, my friend." A faint smile appeared, and he patted Daniel's cheek before pulling him into an embrace. "I couldn't be happier for you." After pounding his friend's back twice, he released Eliakim and hurried off to collect his tool belt before emotions grew too unwieldy.

At work in my household? What a strange thought. Perhaps Eliakim meant the LORD was working to create their child inside Jerusha. Daniel certainly couldn't say he'd experienced Yahweh in any personal way. No burning bush like Moses or visions like Queen Zibah's abba Isaiah.

Tying his leather belt around his waist and repositioning his shoulder bag full of food, he used the flint stones beside the entrance to light a clay lamp. He ducked under the lintel and started his descent into the tunnel, carefully placing one sandal sideways on each of the rock-hewn steps. His broad shoulders nearly touched the walls on both sides. The air was cool but clammy. Metal clanged in the distance. The darkness felt like a sea and the flicker of his lamp the only beacon. This was his world. This, his comfort.

He released his distinctive whistle again, shrill and brief. One, two, three whistles answered in return. Jonah, Nadab, and Reuben were still hard at work with their men. Each foreman had honed a unique trilling to distinguish their individual crews. At dawn, Eliakim would send a man to relieve the night's workers, and three new foremen would report with fresh men to work all day.

Deeper now in the narrowing shaft, Daniel puffed out his lamp and let the weight of utter darkness press on him like a wet, woolen blanket. His other senses sprang to life when sight no longer guided. Smoke from the lamp's smoldering wick mingled with the scent of moist earth. *Ping, ping, ping.* The melody of hammer and chisel drew him forward, holding the lamp in one hand and extending the other to position himself with the wall. His abba had taught him to maneuver caves and tunnels with his mind's eye, using other faculties to *see* himself in the space.

Ping, ping, ping. Continuing forward, Daniel noticed the sound seemed softer, not louder. He whistled again and received his three foremen's replies—louder indeed. Now, he saw a faint light in the distance, and he knew they were ahead of him. Their picks and chisels sang on the mountain's bedrock, but the gentle pings he'd heard had disappeared.

"Silence!" he shouted, barely a hundred paces from the tunnels end. Thirty men stood in dim lamplight, poised like statues, eyes wide. *Nothing*. The pinging was gone. Daniel turned to retrace his steps, hoping to find the exact location of its source.

"Wait!" Nadab grabbed one of their lamps and hurried toward him. "Did you hear cracking?"

"No, no." Daniel said loud enough for all to hear. "There's no sign of weakness in the walls, but I need silence while I check on something."

The men's shoulders relaxed, and their whispered conversation ushered Nadab to Daniel's side. "What are we checking?" He fell into step, eager to help.

Daniel suppressed an impatient reply. He puffed out the lamp's flame. "I don't have time to teach." Daniel kept walking though he heard Nadab gasp at the darkness and his footsteps halt. "Just listen and put your hand on one side of the wall to guide yourself." The shuffling of sandals began behind him, and to the younger man's credit, he remained silent though moving through complete absence of light. Daniel moved more quickly, straining to hear.

Ping.

"There!" He stopped to listen more closely. *Ping, ping.*

Nadab nearly knocked him to the ground. "What are you doing?"

"Listen!" Daniel clamped Nadab's shoulder, afraid his heart was pounding too loud to hear anything else. *Ping, ping.*

"I hear it!" Nadab grabbed Daniel's robe. "It must be the other tunnel crew, but . . ." More silence interrupted by the hope of success. "It sounds like they're above us."

Daniel agreed. "Go back and tell our crews to stop digging.

I'll return to Eliakim, and we'll inspect the other tunnel. Perhaps if we dig up and they dig down, we'll somehow meet." Hand still on Nadab's shoulder, he gave it a good-natured squeeze. "Go!"

Even without a lamp, the man hurried away, the sound of footsteps slapping the rocky path fading as Daniel rushed in the opposite direction. *Yahweh, will You truly give me a baby and connect the king's tunnel in the same day?* Of course, there was still much to fear with the Assyrians bearing down on Judah, but Daniel hadn't had a boost in faith like this since—well, ever.

Three

"The king of Assyria exacted from Hezekiah king of Judah three hundred talents of silver and thirty talents of gold. So Hezekiah gave him all the silver that was found in the temple of the Lord and in the treasuries of the royal palace. At this time Hezekiah king of Judah stripped off the gold with which he had covered the doors and doorposts of the temple of the Lord, and gave it to the king of Assyria."
2 Kings 18:13-16

Jerusha

I startled awake at the knock on my door and wiped a little drool from the corner of my mouth. The midwife said the first few months of any pregnancy were extra tiring, but I'd nodded off like an old woman.

"Coming!" I scurried to my feet, still agile enough to curl my legs beneath me, but winced at a sharp pain low in my belly. "Just a moment." I pressed on the spot and squeezed my eyes closed while the pain passed. *Yahweh, should I be alarmed?* I didn't want to be one of those women who sought out the midwife at every little twinge, but neither did I want to be reckless.

The pain now gone, I drew in a deep breath and gingerly crossed the distance to the door. I opened it to my neighbor and best friend. "Shalom, Bekira."

"What's wrong?" Her eyes went directly to the hand still resting on my belly. "Should I get the midwife?"

I wrapped her shoulders and pulled her inside, closing the door behind us. "I'm perfectly fine." I hoped it was true.

"You look tired, and you were holding your bel—"

"Daniel came home for a late-night visit, and I dozed off while grinding grain." I pointed to the reed mat beside the hand mill and a loaf's worth of flour that I'd spilled on our tiled floor.

"I remember those first months of pregnancy." Bekira's tone was maternal as she placed my fallen hand mill on the low-lying table, while carrying her own basket. "Every woman is exhausted until the mid-point of pregnancy. Then you get a little energy—until the last two months."

I salvaged the flour that hadn't touched the floor, and swept my ruined efforts into a wooden dust shovel. "I plan to enjoy every stage of this miracle, Bekira. Who knows if I'll ever conceive again?"

She set aside Eliakim's morning meal and retrieved an empty basket from my corner to begin packing Daniel's. We'd started the routine months ago, and our friendship had grown through our husbands' long work hours and the short walk to the tunnel site.

After wrapping the last hunk of cheese in a cloth, we gathered our baskets and hurried into the Upper City's pre-dawn streets. Glancing in all directions to be sure no one else heard me, I ventured a whisper. "Has Eliakim said any more about the Assyrians' approach?"

"I haven't seen him since you and I talked at last night's meal," she said. "What did Daniel say about the tunnel?"

How much should I tell her? Technically, her husband was

Daniel's supervisor—even though they were best friends. "He was discouraged, but I think telling him about the baby boosted his faith."

She reached over to pat my tummy. "Children have a way of strengthening our faith and *testing* it." With good-natured laughter, she told me about their youngest daughter's latest antics. The curly-red-haired cherub not only looked like her abba, but she also had Eliakim's sharp mind. "Sometimes I think she's smarter than me," Bekira sighed. "And she's only seven!"

Approaching the tunnel canopy, I noticed Bekira squinting as if to see more clearly through the morning haze. "I don't see Eliakim. Where could he be?" We sped our pace and arrived at Eliakim's familiar workspace: a table littered with drawings, several empty cups, a few wax tablets bearing records, and a basket still half-full of food.

But no Eliakim.

"Perhaps he's gone to the palace," I offered, watching her concern grow.

"We would have heard the shofar if Hezi called a council meeting."

"Maybe the king sent a messenger for Eliakim alone." He and King Hezekiah had been friends since they were boys. "Doesn't the king call for him personally sometimes?"

"Of course, but Eli always sends a messenger to tell me when he leaves the site. He knows I fear he'll go into that tunnel and—" She stopped herself. "Aren't you afraid someday one of the wells or cisterns or tunnels Daniel digs will collapse while he's in it?"

"I used to be," I said. "But my husband is very good at what he does and knows the signs of danger." I placed a finger on one of the drawings lying on the table. "Like your husband has proven himself reliable to the king as a builder, I have complete confidence in Daniel as a digger."

A war raged on Bekira's features, doubt and fear battled

hope and confusion. She turned toward the tunnel entrance. "Maybe he's gone in . . ." She took a step toward the yawning hole in the mountain.

"No, Bekira!" I clamped her shoulder. "We're not allowed—"

She shrugged off my hand. "I'll yell inside. Eliakim will answer if he's in there."

I watched her go, shaking my head but remaining silent. She was too stubborn to persuade. And what if she was right? Maybe Eliakim stepped inside because there was exciting news to share.

"Eliakim!" Bekira shouted into the tunnel. "Can you hear me?"

We waited. Nothing.

She looked back at me, lifted the corner of her mouth and one shoulder. I thought she might give up. Not Bekira.

"Eliakim ben Hilkiah, if you don't answer me, I'm coming in there!"

"Bekira, no! Both our husbands have forbidden us to—"

"Indeed we have." The male voice startled us both. I whirled and nearly bumped noses with Eliakim who stood beneath his canopy. Daniel was beside him, grinning.

"It's daylight. What are you doing outside the tunnel?" I rushed toward my husband and stumbled the last step, his basket of food still jostling on my arm.

He caught me, all humor gone. "Jerusha, be careful. What if you fell?" His bristly tone seemed to shock even him. Softening the harsh lines of his features, he bent to kiss my nose. "You must protect my son."

"Your son, is it?" I whispered.

"Jerusha is with child, Eliakim." Bekira arrived just then, trying to distract from her plight. "Isn't it wonderful?"

"It is good news." Eliakim pulled her into his arms. "But right now I'm more interested in knowing if you would have gone into that tunnel had we not arrived."

I pressed my cheek against Daniel's chest, wishing we could give our friends more privacy, but Daniel seemed anxious to hear her answer.

"Yes, but only because it was so odd for you to be away." Bekira didn't sound at all repentant. I glanced up and saw that she faced her husband, hands balled into fists on her hips. "What could possibly be important enough for you to leave the tunnel entrance without sending a messenger to tell me? You're the one who set the safety precautions that every digger's family must know his location at all times."

"And before this day is out," Eliakim spoke with an unusually sharp tone, "I'll have to send a message to every digger's family to let them know—" He looked at Daniel. "Would you like to tell our wives what that message must say?" A slow grin proved his harshness a trick.

Daniel braced my shoulders, delight dancing in his dark brown eyes. "I think we'll connect the tunnels by nightfall."

My mouth fell open, but before I could shout for joy, my husband snatched me off the ground and twirled me like a child's toy. I buried my giggles in his neck and reveled in his laughter, treasuring it as a gift. *Thank You, Yahweh. Our faith is a flame!* Our God had answered our prayers, and I hoped my husband saw it too.

When he set my feet on the ground, Eliakim and Bekira were much more subdued, their heads bent together in quiet conversation. I watched their expressions, and it didn't seem Eliakim was angry—more so afraid.

"Has something else happened with the Assyrians?" I asked, pressing myself closer to Daniel's side.

Eliakim's gaze lingered on his wife, and she nodded, seemingly a silent prod. With a deep sigh, he reached for her hand and turned to Daniel and me. "The Assyrians have crossed our northern border. They've already taken some of the smaller towns and villages and will likely reach Jerusalem within two days. The king has decided to pay the tribute we owe them—that's gone unpaid for years."

My face felt prickly, as if a thousand insects lit on my cheeks. "Does he have that kind of wealth in Jerusalem's treasury?"

Eliakim shook his head. "He's ordered the priests to strip the gold and silver from Yahweh's Temple—"

"Like his pagan abba, King Ahaz." Daniel finished the sentence, drawing a heated stare from his friend.

"Hezi isn't his abba."

Daniel inclined his head in respect. "I agree. King Hezekiah is a righteous man, and I'm sure he's doing what he believes Yahweh wishes."

Something shadowed Eliakim's countenance at Daniel's words. Was it doubt? Perhaps sadness. "This morning," he said, "I'll address all of Jerusalem and ask our citizens for help."

"What kind of help?" I asked.

"We need the citizens of Jerusalem to venture outside our walls and spoil as many nearby springs and wells as possible."

"Spoil our people's water supply?" Daniel asked. "How does that make sense when we've put all this labor into bringing outside water into the city?"

"We'll protect the Gihon Spring," Eliakim said. "Camouflage it so the Assyrians don't know it's there. But other water sources outside our gates will become water for our enemies when they attack us. We must fill wells with dirt and reroute springs to hide them, providing Assyria with as little water as possible during a siege."

"That's brilliant." I couldn't think of anything else to say—except, "I want to help."

"No!" Daniel gripped my arm. "You're not leaving this city."

Shocked, I stared into the face of a man I hardly knew. My husband never made demands. Because he was away for work so much, I made most decisions myself. When he returned, we discussed decisions and made them together. "I love you, Daniel ben Josiah because you're a man of honor. You risk your life every day for our people, picking at rocks under the weight of mountains. So when I'm asked to walk a few furlongs and dump a bucket or two of dirt into a well, I'm going to take that risk." I raised a single eyebrow, daring him to challenge me.

"But what if . . ." His eyes pleaded, conveying the words he couldn't speak.

"This child is Yahweh's. Our lives are Yahweh's. Trusting this truth is the only way I let you leave me day after day."

"I'll go with her." Bekira circled my waist and looked at my husband.

Daniel's breaths grew labored, his brow downturned. He turned his attention to Eliakim. "Why can't you take some of the tunneling crews off project now that we're close? Or use soldiers to ruin the water sources outside the city."

Eliakim started shaking his head before Daniel finished. "We need every man of the king's forced labor to finish the tunnels, and our army must hold the Assyrians off as long as possible. It falls to the citizens inside our walls, my friend." He pulled Bekira to his side and kissed her forehead. "We should be proud of our wives, Daniel."

"We'll be the first ones out of the gates." Bekira promised. "We'll go to the closest source and no farther. And I promise we'll run into the city at the first hint of trouble."

Daniel stared at the impetuous woman for more than a heartbeat before turning my chin to meet his gaze. "Bekira was ready to descend into that tunnel entrance against her husband's wishes." One side of his mouth curved into a grin, and he placed his hand on my belly. "Make sure our child, you, and Eliakim's wife return safely. I have more confidence in *your* sense than hers."

Four

*"But if you say to me, 'We are depending on the Lord our God'—
isn't he the one whose high places and altars Hezekiah removed,
saying to Judah and Jerusalem,
'You must worship before this altar in Jerusalem?'"*
2 Kings 18:22

Jerusha

Bekira and I hurried home, explaining as little of the danger as possible to her three children before taking her only son with us. Jahleel was happy to join us, escaping from his older sister's charge. Bekira's oldest could watch the youngest girl while we joined others of Jerusalem's faithful to sabotage every well and spring within a morning's walk of our gates.

"Why must we walk through the Lower City?" Jahleel's adolescent whine rubbed my raw nerves, but Bekira answered with an ima's teaching tone.

"It's the quickest way to En Rogel and, remember, no complaining. You know what happened when our ancestors complained after the exodus from Egypt." The eleven-year-old rolled his eyes, but he stopped whining. Few traversed the southern city without a good reason. Built on Jerusalem's downward slope, all refuse drained through its central street, and most of the city's industry stank of it.

As we neared the southernmost city gate, my friend turned to me. "We'll arrive at En Rogel first. Others can walk to farther wells and springs." Her lips pursed together. "I suppose we should have brought shovels. Didn't Eli say we needed to reroute a spring and camouflage it?" With a shrug of her shoulder, she dismissed the thought. "We'll wait for others to join us at the spring. Surely, they'll bring extra tools."

I tried not to laugh, but was unsuccessful. "I thought you knew what we were doing. This is so like you, Bekira—to rush into the fray and ask questions later."

She linked her arm with mine and the other with Jahleel's. "Who needs shovels when we have three brilliant minds? We'll dig with our hands if needed."

Jahleel slid his arm away from hers. "You lied about the Assyrians, Ima." He picked up some small stones and threw them at self-appointed targets. "We're spoiling the En Rogel spring so they won't have water while we're locked inside Jerusalem's walls." He hurled a rock at an innocent scrub bush.

Bekira and I exchanged a glance. "Are you frightened?" I asked. It was the first question that came to mind.

"I'm more angry than afraid. If I was a year older, I could have been trained for battle and marched out with the army." Bekira turned away, her sniffing proof she was grateful for his youth.

"I'm scared," I admitted. "Master Daniel and I are having a baby, Jahleel, and we want our child to grow up with the freedoms you've enjoyed under King Hezekiah's reign."

He peeked at me shyly. "I hope it's a boy. Then I can teach him how to use a sling—"

"Oh!" I grabbed at the sudden cramp in my abdomen.

"Are you all right?" Bekira's hand was on my back, concern pinching her mouth like a raisin.

Yahweh, this is the second time today I've felt this. Should I go home? The pain eased immediately, and though I saw no burning bush or rainbow in the sky, I felt the affirming peace of my God. "I'm fine," I said to my friend. "I must have pulled a muscle this morning when I stood too quickly."

Bekira looked at me as if scolding a child. "You can pull a muscle in your leg or hip, but you're not allowed any sort of pain in your tummy while pregnant." She winked and offered her arm to steady me. "Let's help each other climb the hill to the spring."

"And perhaps slow our pace," I suggested, resting my hand on her arm.

For the remainder of our journey, even Jahleel treated me like Persian pottery. We were first to arrive at the spring, as Bekira hoped, but realized digging with our hands was impractical. Though not a gushing spring, En Rogel produced enough water to flow over rocks and leave a small but visible trail of mud down the hillside. We splashed our feet in the bubbling source and waited for others to arrive.

"Did you come to work or play?" A gruff male voice called out.

Dripping wet, we all three stilled as if we'd been caught stealing warm bread before a meal. An old man climbed the hillside, leading a donkey and two boys close to Jahleel's age.

"A little of both." I splashed Jahleel once more for mischief's sake.

He retaliated, but Bekira stopped us both with a stern glance. "I see you've brought tools and two good helpers. We don't have shovels, but we came to work."

The man slapped his donkey's backside as if he wished it were one of us and whispered something to the two boys with him. When the newcomers arrived at the spring head, each of the boys grabbed a hoe and walked away without a word of greeting. About fifteen paces east, they began hacking at the ground near a copse of trees as if it had offended them.

"I'm Levi," the old man said, "and those are my grandsons." He pulled two shovels from the donkey's pack and handed them to Jahleel and me. "You two start here at the spring and dig along the tree line toward my boys. We'll divert the spring to the east and gently downhill and hide it with the brush along the tree line."

"You have no more tools." Bekira's hands were on her hips again. "What will you and I do?"

His reply was both a grunt and chuckle. "We let the young ones dig until they're tired, and then we old ones give them a rest."

"I'm not old—"

"When you get tired," he shouted at his grandsons, "Mistress Bekira or I will dig until you're rested."

Bekira shot a puzzled glance at me. *How did he know my name?*

The boys paused their hacking. One of them grinned. "We don't get tired, Saba." When they returned to their task, Levi raised a bristly brow at me. "I suppose you're the only one who will need my help today." Something strange simmered in his rheumy brown eyes. I started digging to avoid his gaze.

"It's like Abba's tunnel," Jahleel said, already at work. "We'll dig from the spring; your grandsons will start at the other end; and we'll meet in the middle."

"Your Abba is a fine man." Levi patted Jahleel's shoulder and turned his focus on Bekira. "I've known Lord Eliakim since he was a boy."

"How exactly do you know my husband's family?"

I let their conversation fade to the edge of my consciousness, giving full attention to digging—and Assyria's imminent attack. If Eliakim was right, King Sennacherib's army would surround Jerusalem in two days. Though most had never endured a siege, everyone knew of Assyria's three-year siege against Samaria,

Israel's capital. Everyone knew, but not everyone prepared. The same people who called Daniel odd also deemed me compulsive. But when the Assyrians camped outside our walls, who would they ask to share supplies? I'd spent the past three months stocking dried fish, dried fruit, and nuts. How long it lasted would depend on the number of hungry neighbors at our door.

Jahleel rammed his shovel into the earth as if stabbing an enemy. "Everyone in Jerusalem respects my abba." The boy sounded defensive, so I perked my ears to the conversation.

"I agree," the old man said, "but someone can be respected and still have enemies."

The boy emptied the dirt from his shovel, leaned on the handle, and looked at Levi. "I know what Lord Isaiah prophesied about Abba. He said, 'All the responsibility of our family will hang on him like clothes on a wooden peg. He'll be like an abba to the whole city of Jerusalem. But someday the peg will be sheared off and everyone hanging on him will fall when he falls.' That's what Yahweh says about my abba." Tears gathered on his lashes, and I thought my heart would break.

Bekira looked haunted, and she grabbed him in a ferocious hug. "Who told you about Lord Isaiah's prophecy?" I'd hoped she would deny it.

He lifted his arms, as if they were iron, and circled her waist. "I heard you and Abba talking about it when you thought we were sleeping." He pulled away and met his ima's startled gaze. "Do you think the Assyrians are the ones who will cut Abba off and make us fall?"

"No." Levi's definitive answer stole our attention. "No, Jahleel. Your abba will be Jerusalem's hero. He and Daniel will finish King Hezekiah's tunnel, and your abba will show both his courage and his faith throughout Assyria's attack."

Bekira stepped between Levi and her son, brow furrowed. "I appreciate your encouragement, Levi, I pray your words are true. However, it seems unwise to speak with such certainty about things we can't possibly—"

"Let's make sure the Assyrians never find the En Rogel spring," I interrupted. The old man had done nothing to make us afraid, yet I felt it unwise to contradict him. "Our trench is taking shape, Bekira. Perhaps you and Levi could begin gathering scrub to hide it." With the next stab of my shovel, I pressed my foot down on the shovel's head, and a wrenching pain shot through my abdomen. Wailing, I doubled over in pain.

"Jerusha!" Bekira bent over me. "Are you all right?"

But I couldn't answer. Couldn't think or breathe. Falling to my knees, I could only push out a sound between clenched teeth. "Zzzzhhhh."

"Jahleel, go get the midwife and our carriage!"

I shook my head violently. *I can't lose our baby, Yahweh! Please!*

"A carriage will take too long." Levi swept me into his arms and gently placed me on his donkey. "You are the one who needs my help today," he whispered.

By the time my pain lessened, we were on our way down the gentle slope toward the city. My legs hung over one side, and Bekira walked on the other to steady me. "What about Jahleel?"

"He will stay and dig with my boys." Levi's answer felt like a command.

"Bekira?" Was she at all uncomfortable with this stranger?

"Daniel will kill me," she mumbled. "I should never have let you come."

"It's not your fault. If anyone was to blame, I should have known the pains weren't simply a strained muscle."

"It's silly to cast blame," Levi said over his shoulder. "Someone very wise once said, 'The child is Yahweh's. Our lives are Yahweh's.' It's good to remember calm wisdom when fear causes frenzied thoughts."

Bekira's hand stilled on my back. Though I couldn't see her, I knew she recognized my words from Levi's mouth: *The child is Yahweh's. Our lives are Yahweh's.* I'd said it to Daniel at the tunnel site earlier in the day, but no one except Bekira and Eliakim could have heard it. *Yahweh, are we in the presence of Your angel or Your enemy?* My belly tightened with another contraction, and I groaned, praying with new fervency. *Yahweh, protect my baby. Protect Bekira, Jahleel, and me. And, LORD, answer the pleading I can't even form into words!*

FIVE

> *"Then Isaiah son of Amoz sent a message to Hezekiah: 'This is what the Lord, the God of Israel, says: I have heard your prayer concerning Sennacherib king of Assyria. This is the word that the Lord has spoken against him: "...He will not enter this city or shoot an arrow here. He will not come before it with shield or build a siege ramp against it. By the way that he came he will return."'"*
> **2 Kings 19:20-21; 32-33**

JERUSHA

I laid perfectly still in the fading darkness on the straw-stuffed mattress Bekira had given me three days ago. It had been three days since I scurried into the city with Levi. Three days since I'd seen Daniel. Three days since I'd sensed Yahweh's presence.

Three days.

Why have You forsaken me? Why are You so far away? I cry out, but You don't answer. I groan, but You're silent.

I feel nothing. Neither the pain that terrified nor the peace that buoyed me. At least there's no more bleeding. Cramping returns if I stand. With the slightest weight on my feet, my abdomen squeezes like a mercilessly tightening belt.

Bekira wanted to send for Daniel. I wouldn't allow it. She took his meals twice a day and left them with Eliakim to deliver. The men didn't question my absence since tunnel complications stole their attention. The tunnels should have merged by now.

Should have. It was a dangerous place to dwell.

I should have stayed in the city like Daniel told me. I should have known the pains weren't strained muscles. I should have divorced Daniel years ago, freeing him to marry a wife who could bear him children.

"Jerusha!" My husband's excited voice echoed off stone walls. "Jerusha, we've done it! We've merged the tunnels!"

I could feign sleep, but his shouting would betray the deception.

He slapped aside our bedchamber curtain and gasped when he saw Levi lying on a mat beside me. "Who are you?" Suddenly defensive, his eyes reflected the flame of a single lamp. He shot a confused glance at me and back at Levi, whose languid stretching only enraged him more. "What is this stranger doing in our bedchamber?"

"I'm Levi." He stood, offering his hand in greeting. "Congratulations on completing the tunnel, Daniel. Those last few vertical cubits were tricky, weren't they?" He clasped my husband's shoulder and chuckled as he walked past him into our main room.

Daniel stood in the doorway, gawking, looking to me for answers.

"I think he's sent from Yahweh," I said, "but I have no guess why he's here." I turned to face the wall. "I've been in bed for three days, Daniel. It's likely I'll lose the baby."

"What?" He crossed the room and draped himself across my back. "Why didn't you send for me?"

The quaver in his voice cut me to the core. "I'm sorry,

Daniel. You had such good news. I shouldn't have—"

"You *should* have sent for me right away." He gently rolled me over to meet his pained expression. "The tunnel wasn't more important than my wife and child."

I wanted to throw my arms around his neck and surrender to his comfort. But what was the point? "What could you have done, Daniel? There's nothing to do but wait. Wait on Assyria to attack. Wait on our child to die."

"No!" His arms slid beneath me, pulling me tightly to his chest. "We will not lose hope, Jerusha. *You* will not lose hope." His arms slackened, and he cradled me in front of him. "Who was that old man—Levi? Is he the one filling your head with doubt?"

I almost laughed. "Levi only repeats my own words to me. *The child is Yahweh's. Our lives are Yahweh's.*" How could I explain the unique relationship we had forged? "Bekira and I met him when we went to En Rogel. We knew right away he was . . . different."

"What do you mean different?"

"He knew Bekira's name without being told."

"Jerusalem is an ancient city with deep family roots. It's not uncommon—"

"Daniel." My tone silenced him. "He *knew* things. Even before my labor started, he told me he'd come to the spring to help me. When the pain started, he lifted me onto his donkey like I weighed less than a sack of grain."

"All right, so Levi is different." His deep sigh betrayed the bone-deep weariness of the good man I'd married. "Please, Jerusha. Give me some logical reason you didn't send for me when your labor began and find a better explanation for the stranger I found sitting by your bed."

I choked on a cynical laugh and shook my head. "I know it sounds crazy, but—" New clarity began to dawn. "What if Levi *is* Yahweh's presence with me, Daniel?" I raised on one elbow to call out. "Levi, are you still here? Levi!"

"Yes, yes, I'm here. Stop your squawking." The old man entered with a tray of food. He set it beside the mattress and sat himself beside Daniel. "Yahweh most certainly sent me and my grandsons to En Rogel. Your wife needed help, and Mistress Bekira has cared for my boys while I continued helping Jerusha in your absence."

"But I would have come home if I'd known—"

Levi lifted one hand for silence. "Yahweh didn't want you to come home. You and Eliakim were the only ones capable of connecting those tunnels, but I was more than capable of caring for your wife. Now, my work is done." He swiped his hands together twice. "I'll collect my grandsons and go home."

He leaned on one arm to stand, but Daniel halted his progress with a whisper. "Are you an angel from Yahweh?"

He grinned, his rheumy eyes focused on Daniel. "Have I given you a message?" Daniel didn't answer, so he explained, "An angel is God's messenger and always comes with a word from the Throne." Levi stood as if to go but paused in the doorway. "I'm sorry neither of you were able to attend the special worship at Yahweh's Temple last night. King Hezekiah announced Isaiah's most recent prophecy." He closed his eyes as if reading from a scroll in his mind. "Thus says the LORD, the God of Abraham, Isaac, and Jacob: 'Because Sennacherib raged against Me and because his insolence has reached My ears, I will put My hook in his nose and My bit in his mouth, and I will make him return by the way he came.'" He opened his eyes, and with another grin added, "You'll have quite a story to tell your little boy." Slipping around the curtain, he was gone.

Daniel stared at me, dazed. "Did he just deliver a message from Yahweh?"

"Or was he repeating Isaiah's prophecy and adding a hopeful blessing?" I laughed and melted into my husband's embrace, feeling sweet peace. Whatever Levi had done, whoever he was, he'd given us an invaluable parting gift.

Six

"But the people remained silent and said nothing in reply, because the king had commanded, 'Do not answer him.'"
2 Kings 18:36

Daniel

Cloaked in heavy darkness, Daniel pressed both hands against the tunnel's side walls. Vibrations began slowly but intensified. Deeper into the earth. Louder all around him. The wall cracked under one hand and then the other. "Rockburst!" he shouted, but no one replied. He was alone. The pounding vibrations shook him. He'd be buried under the mountain alone. "No. Nooo!" Bolting upright, dripping sweat and panting, he sat beside Jerusha.

"I'm here, Daniel." She hung on his shoulder. "It was only a dream."

Eyes closed, he still sensed a vibration. This one beneath him. It wasn't a dream. He shot to his feet, shouting as he ran toward the door. "The Assyrians are here, Jerusha." A trumpet call overshadowed his words, guiding him to Yahweh's Temple.

Thankful he wasn't in the tunnel, he'd hear this report in person.

Among the first to arrive, Daniel climbed the Temple's northern portico. The southern balcony was reserved for the king's family and the east porch for nobility. Daniel and his abba held more wealth than most nobles but never cared to mingle. In fact, he usually stood among the common folk in the Outer Courts, but he took his seat in the portico, grateful for the bird's-eye view.

"We don't have much time," the high priest announced to the gathering throng. "Please remain quiet and gather closely so there's room for as many citizens as possible to hear the king's instructions." People spilled through the entrances, filling every open space, like an overturned pitcher soaking dry ground. Only shuffling footsteps stirred the terrified silence.

Daniel dipped his head, greeting a neighbor and his wife who filed in beside him. The man's shoulder pressed against his, forcing Daniel against the stone pillar at the end of the row. He closed his eyes, imagining himself in the tunnel. Alone. The quiet helped, but his skin crawled with the sounds of breathing. The stench of stale sweat and foul breath. Someone had eaten onions and garlic to break their fast. *Yahweh, keep me calm.* If he panicked, he could unintentionally hurt someone with his bulk. Placing a hand over his nose and mouth, he'd be better off smelling his own foul breath than others'.

Rippling whispers started at the royal's side of the gathering and spread toward him. Daniel opened his eyes. King Hezekiah entered with Eliakim instead of Queen Zibah this morning. *Unusual.* The king raised his hands, silencing the whispers.

"Thank you for answering the trumpet's call so quickly. We return to Yahweh's Dwelling this morning after praising Him here last night for His promised deliverance from Assyria. Is it coincidence that our enemy arrives at dawn?" He waited, but no one spoke. "Is it coincidence that our enemy knows I destroyed the high places where Judeans worshiped Yahweh?"

Hushed conversation spread throughout the audience. The king had destroyed *all* high places, it was true, including those supposedly dedicated to Yahweh. But those truly faithful knew those same altars were also used for pagan rites.

"I destroyed them because Yahweh commanded Moses that we worship in one place, in His one Dwelling Place. Here." He paused, looking into individual faces of those in the crowd. "I ask you, good people of Jerusalem, how did Assyria's king know of my actions?"

Not a sound. Prickly flesh crawled up Daniel's arms.

"There are spies among us. Assyrian weasels who want to destroy your trust in me *and* your trust in Yahweh." He pounded his chest with his fist. "But I implore you, don't let them!"

"We won't!" A man shouted from the courtyard.

"The Assyrians will promise lies, but they can't divide us." Hezi pounded his chest again. "They will shout threats, but they can't divide us. They will use trickery and terror to defeat us before they ever draw their swords. But I command you, people of Jerusalem, chosen children of God Most High. Do. Not. Speak. No one inside these walls is to reply. We will let this man, the man who brought water into our city, speak for us all!" He raised Eliakim's hand like a victor.

The crowd's cheer rose to the heavens, shaking the very foundation of Yahweh's Temple. Daniel covered his ears but kept his eyes open and even smiled. Yes, this was worth watching. Worth celebrating in the face of Jerusalem's testing. Their righteous king and Daniel's dearest friend would lead them against the world's greatest army—and Yahweh would give them victory.

Both Eliakim and the king knelt before the high priest, who signaled the Levitical choir to sing one of David's psalms. Resonant, bass voices lifted praise to El Shaddai, and Daniel noticed for the first time a young scribe sitting cross-legged at the Temple gate. He scribbled furiously on parchment, while a sour-faced man in purple robes stood beside him. Arms crossed, Shebna—the man Eliakim replaced as palace administrator—watched in silence. Though Eliakim seldom mentioned his palace responsibilities while they worked on the tunnel, Daniel often noticed the inner battles written on his friend's face. More than once Daniel had proven a confidant for Eliakim to rage about Shebna's evils.

When Daniel had last seen his friend at the tunnel before dawn, they'd shared unbridled joy that Yahweh used human hands to miraculously connect a spring with a cistern. Spanning less time than a soldier's watch, Eliakim now seemed to carry the weight of Judah on his shoulders. *Yahweh, Eliakim lives to serve You. Protect him while he's caught between political boulders and grinding wheels.*

By the time Daniel returned from the Temple, the noise was unbearable. The barbarians spiked Judean prisoners on poles, higher than the city walls, surrounding Jerusalem with torture and death. Daniel had always enjoyed having their family home nestled beside Jerusalem's eastern wall.

Not today. The arrival of Assyria's troops brought true *war* to Jerusalem.

The tortured cries grew louder with every pole added to the Assyrian's garden of death. He flung open his courtyard gate, hurried into the house, and went straight to the bedchamber—but halted at the doorway. Jerusha sat on her mattress, eating a bowl of gruel.

"Where did you get that? Should you be sitting?" He sounded like a nagging wife.

Startled, she set the gruel aside. "Bekira's daughter delivered it, and I haven't had any pain. I must try things and find out what I can and can't do."

"Can I trust you to tell me if you have pain?" He marched toward her like a sentry.

She looked down, picking at her fingers. "I don't keep secrets from you, Daniel." Her voice was small. He'd hurt her.

Dragging fingers through his hair, he sat next to her and stilled her fidgeting hands. "I'm sorry. I know you don't keep secrets. It's the noise. I—" He motioned toward the window and then to his ear. "I think it's somehow louder in my head than others hear it. I can't pretend it's not there."

She placed her hand on his cheek, eyes filling with tears. "I forget sometimes that you experience things more intensely." Pointing beyond the curtain, she said, "Would you bring my basket of bandages and ointments? I think I can help."

He would appease his wife, though certain Jerusha's bandages and ointments couldn't help the poor souls tortured on Assyrian pikes. Retrieving the large basket from a shelf in the main room, he placed it beside his wife and watched as she tore pieces of cloth from a rolled bandage. Then, wadding them into balls, she motioned him toward her. "Lean closer."

He laughed, realizing she was about to stuff the cloth in his ears. A terrifying conversation stole his attention. "Wait!" He seized her hands. "Eliakim is outside the wall!" Daniel stood on the mattress to peek out the small window at the valley far below. He could see only the soldiers' encampment, but his friend's words were clear.

"Please, speak in Aramaic rather than Hebrew in the hearing of the people on the walls."

But Sennacherib's general continued his taunting in Hebrew. "Is it only you and your king who will drink urine and eat dung during this siege? Hear the word of the great king of Assyria: 'Do not let Hezekiah deceive you, citizens of Jerusalem! Hezekiah can't deliver you from my hand. Don't let him persuade you to trust in Yahweh. Don't listen when he says, "The Lord will deliver us." Make peace with me. Then you will eat fruit from your own vine and fig tree and drink water from your own cistern. I will come and take you to a land like your own—a land of grain and new wine, a land of bread and vineyards, a land of olive trees and honey.'"

Jerusha covered her ears. "Will the people listen to his lies? Will they call for surrender?"

"No." Daniel rose to his tip-toes, looking farther south. "The king told us not to answer, no matter what the Assyrians said." He still couldn't see the negotiating party.

"The great King Sennacherib says, 'Choose life and not death,'" the Rabshakeh continued. "Hezekiah is misleading you when he says, 'The Lord will deliver us.' Has the god of any nation ever delivered his land from my hand? Where are the gods of Hamath and Arpad? Where are the gods of Sepharvaim, Hena and Ivvah? Did they rescue Samaria from my hand? Who of all the gods of these countries has been able to save his land? How then can Yahweh deliver Jerusalem?"

Daniel looked down and saw a stream of tears running down Jerusha's cheeks. He left the window and pulled her into his lap, wrapping his arms and legs around her, cocooning her inside a shell of faith. "Listen to me. Last night's worship sealed Isaiah's promise from Yahweh that Jerusalem will be saved, and this morning our righteous king gave instruction for us to stand silent against Assyria's lies. I don't know how, Jerusha, but our God will save this city. We must trust. We *will* trust." She trembled, and his own body shook uncontrollably despite his brave words. *Please, Yahweh. You've bolstered my faith. I truly believe You'll deliver us. Please don't betray me.*

"Oooh." Jerusha clutched at her belly. "I need to lie flat." She clawed at the mattress to lie down, taking deep breaths, her face pinched in pain.

Terror shot through him. "What can I do?"

She took a deep breath and released it slowly. When she opened her eyes, her brows lifted. "It wasn't as bad as I feared, and it stopped quickly. Maybe my womb will heal, Daniel, and Jerusalem will be saved."

Her lips trembled when she said it, but she was trying to trust. He laid beside her, curling his body around her and pulling her close. "We'll wait right here until our child is stronger and we see Isaiah's words fulfilled. *Assyria will return by the way they came.*"

Seven

> *"Listen! When [the King of Assyria] hears a certain report, I will make him want to return to his own country, and there I will have him cut down with the sword."*
> **2 Kings 19:7**

Jerusha

One Week Later

I lay in my husband's arms, watching Yahweh display His mastery of shading outside our window. How could every starlit night hold unique beauty and every dawn begin on ebony canvas yet splay varied combinations of amethyst, sapphire, jacinth, and topaz? *I will trust the Creator of the moon, sun, and stars to create the new life in me.*

My little warrior had fought a good fight. He—or she—seemed content to wait for a later arrival. No labor pains in two days meant I could at least sit up and even walk occasionally, though Daniel wouldn't let me wander far from my mattress.

Yesterday, I'd convinced him to let me spin a little wool to keep my hands busy.

How long would the Assyrians do nothing? I supposed it was part of their famed mental warfare. They'd driven whole cities to suicide by simply shouting threats and planned torture.

A thin ray of dawn caressed Daniel's cheek, and I wanted to touch it. Touch him. Despite the army camped outside the wall, our week together had been glorious. Always tender, my husband had added compassion to his list of wonders. Not only had he tended to my needs, but he'd also entertained Jahleel when Bekira was frazzled with her son. Though Eliakim's long days at the tunnel were done, endless council meetings at the palace kept him away from a boy who needed his abba—and Daniel had been a good substitute.

My husband grimaced at the brightening light now disturbing his slumber. One eye opened to a slit, and I met it with an eager grin. "Shalom, my love."

He groaned. "Why do you do that?"

"Do what?" How could I offend with three words?

He pulled me into his arms, snuggling like a child with his favorite toy. "Why do you love mornings and stare at me until I wake?"

"I don't do it every morning—do I?" Our laughter felt good. Almost normal.

But sudden commands in Akkadian and thundering hooves brought us both to our feet. He peered out the window, and I pounded his shoulder, too short to see. "What's happening?"

"Hundreds—no thousands—of Assyrians are riding south. But they're leaving their tents and supplies."

"Is this Isaiah's prophecy fulfilled?" Even as I asked, I knew the answer.

"Some soldiers remain with their tents." He turned from the window, shaking his head. "If they fulfilled Isaiah's prophecy, and 'returned the way they came,' Assyria is north."

I hated that he was so logical. "Where could they be going?"

Still shaking his head, he only glanced at me before walking toward the main room. "I'll get something to break our fast."

"Daniel, wait." He stopped at the doorway but didn't face me. "Do you know where they're going?"

"I don't know anything." He whirled on me, his lips pursed in a thin, tight line. "At least when I was digging the tunnel, I was part of a solution, and I knew the plan. Now, I'm nothing, Jerusha. Eliakim is counselor to the king, and I'm Judah's Mole. What I really want to know is what's happening with my friend in that palace."

"But you hate politics," I reminded him. "Do you really want to know what's happening in the palace, or are you simply worried about Eliakim?"

His hands clenched and unclenched while he considered my question. Finally, letting his head fall forward, he released a sigh. "A man needs to feel needed, Jerusha." He looked up at me again. "*And* I want to know if Eliakim is all right."

My heart ached at the battle raging inside him. "I'm sure after your success with the tunnel, the king would place you on his royal council since he asked you to consider it two years ago."

He'd started shaking his head before I finished speaking. "I can't sit in a room, arguing day and night, with arrogant old men."

I couldn't hide my amusement. "I suspect they wouldn't enjoy you either."

"I suppose not." A slight grin brought on a bigger sigh, giving me permission to suggest a less conventional solution.

"I could visit Bekira today and ask if she's heard anything from Eliakim. I'm feeling better, and I'll return right away if the pains return." He didn't refuse, proving how deeply concerned he was.

"All right," he said, "but wait until mid-morning and don't tire yourself." He covered the four strides between us and pulled me into a tight hug. "I wish I could be an eloquent council member or a brave military hero like other husbands, but I'm more comfortable below ground than above it, Jerusha."

I couldn't bear his self-loathing. Cradling his forlorn expression, I stared into the windows of his soul. "Daniel ben Josiah, your eloquence comes with a chisel and hammer, and you used that God-given ability to save this city. You're braver than any man I know, and Lord Eliakim is blessed to call you his friend." I covered his mouth with a kiss before he could argue, reminding him there was one person on earth who believed him a hero.

I stepped into our courtyard and turned my face toward the bright, autumn sun. *Thank You, Yahweh, for giving my child a home in my womb, for letting me enjoy the breeze on my skin, and the fellowship of friends.* Everything was more precious when it teetered on the brink of loss.

My steps light, I continued through our courtyard gate and strolled next door, calling out peace to my nearest and dearest friend. "Shalom, Bekira! Are you home?"

The oak door flung open, and she met me while drying her hands on a ragged cloth. "You're on your feet!" Her embrace was like a woolen blanket on cold nights, as comfortable as it was warm. My friend held me without speaking, and tears came unbidden. She sniffed too. Friendship was a holy thing, and our reunion was long overdue, anointed with sacred tears. I hadn't seen her since Daniel replaced Levi at my bedside.

I was struck by a thought. "Did Levi say goodbye to you before he left Jerusalem?"

She chuckled and led me into her busy home, chatting as she walked. "What makes you think he left Jerusalem?"

"Shalom, Mistress Jerusha." Jahleel hurried past on his way outside.

His ima lifted a basket off the table. "Don't forget to deliver Widow Achsah's bread."

The boy stomped back and snatched it from her hand. "Sorry, Ima."

She ruffled his hair. "Pass along my blessing to Master Levi and the boys."

Stunned, I couldn't even form words for a question. Bekira laughed when she glimpsed my expression. "Don't look so shocked. Levi told us he'd known Eliakim since he was a boy."

"Yes, but I thought—"

"You thought he was an angel from Yahweh?" she snorted, walking around the table to pour more grain into her elder daughter's hand mill. "So did I at first. But angels don't need silver to raise two growing grandsons."

I was here to ask about Eliakim and the Assyrians, but Daniel would be just as interested about Levi. "He asked you for silver?"

"He didn't need to," she said, demonstrating to her youngest daughter how to knead bread. "I knew he needed it because of the street where he lived in the Lower City."

"He told you where he lived?"

My friend slid a bowl of flour, a pitcher of water and another pitcher of oil toward me. "You can work while we talk. I need bread for our meal tonight in addition to what we provide for the hungry." She shoved a small clay bowl filled with salt alongside the other ingredients and waved her hand over it all. "Mix them as you do for your own bread. Yes, I know where Levi lives, and Jahleel is learning to care for those in the Lower City with Levi's help. It's a good thing I think."

"Of course," I said, making the dough. "A very good thing." Could an angel have a home in the Lower City? "Daniel and I are worried about Eliakim."

"We're too honest with each other to hide behind veiled questions, Jerusha." Bekira looked up from kneading and grinned. "You want to know why the Assyrians left this morning."

My cheeks warmed. "It's true. I'm curious about the Assyrians, but Daniel is truly upset. He feels worthless, Bekira. He misses Eliakim and the time they spent working together."

She set aside her dough, painting her cheeks with flour as she pushed stray hairs off her forehead. "You know how much Eliakim and I love Daniel, and I know he wants to help. But he'd hate the council meetings Eliakim endures. He'd go mad with the bickering and political maneuvering."

"I'm not asking for Eliakim to put him on the council." I sighed, sprinkling a little flour on the table to prepare it for kneading my freshly-made dough. "I simply want Eliakim to consider ways Daniel's digging talents might be useful in fighting Assyria." I wiggled my eyebrows with a mischievous grin. "And I'm dying to know about the Assyrians. Where did they go and if they're coming back?"

Bekira's jolly laughter was medicine to my soul. "I only know we've sent a spy to follow the Assyrians, but no one knows why they left so suddenly." With mischief of her own dancing on plump cheeks, she lowered her voice to a conspiratorial whisper. "Maybe your Daniel could tunnel into their camp and find out."

Eight

*"When the field commander heard that the king of Assyria had
left Lachish, he withdrew and
found the king fighting against Libnah."*
2 Kings 19:8

Jerusha

Six Days Later

"But I haven't had any pains in almost a week." Why must a grown woman argue for the right to walk to the Lower City? "Daniel, you're being unreasonable."

"Unreasonable?" Folding his arms across his well-muscled chest, he blocked the door like a sentinel. "The Assyrians came back two days ago and could begin an assault any moment. Am I more *unreasonable* than you, who invited Levi—a total stranger you'd met that morning—to stay with you three days while keeping me in the dark about your labor pains?"

"You like the dark." I grinned, trying to charm him since brawn wouldn't work. His lips twitched, fighting a smile.

"Come with us," I begged. "The commander told Eliakim the Assyrians won't likely attack for a few more days. They're licking their battle wounds from the strange defeat in Libnah."

He lifted a single brow. "Tell me you don't believe the story about the rats. The fiercest army in the world was not defeated by rats gnawing on their leather weapons."

"I don't know what to believe," I said, "but if you come with us to deliver bread, you'll see Levi again. You and Jahleel can be our pack mules. Bekira always bakes too much bread, and she forces all three children to help with deliveries to the poorest of poor in Jerusalem. If you come, Jahleel will be thrilled to spend the day with you, and perhaps the two girls can stay home. All three children will love you forever."

"They already love me." His lips curved into a lopsided grin. "I would like to see Levi a second time. Perhaps he's got wings tucked under his robe or an extra pair of eyes or another head like the cherubim in Isaiah's vision."

"Stop teasing! I think he's an angel, not a cherub." I rushed at him and threw my arms around his neck, but he only hugged me gently. "I miss your whirling hugs."

He kissed the tip of my nose. "I'll give you a whirling hug if you walk to the Lower City without labor pains."

"Agreed." I led him by the hand to Bekira's.

"Did you ask where she's getting the grain?"

I kept my voice low. "She said a 'friend' is supplying it." I raised my brow, hoping he'd draw the same conclusion I had. Levi was almost certainly providing as Elijah had supplied the widow's oil during the drought. People all over Jerusalem were running low on grain.

"Finally! You're here!" Bekira was flitting around her kitchen like a bee in a field of clover. "Daniel, are you coming too?"

He glared at me, brows drawn together, but I knew the tender heart beneath that crusty shell. "He is, and he's happy to take over for the girls if they'd like to stay home and have a free afternoon."

As predicted, Bekira's girls squealed and bowed to their next-door hero. Jahleel offered Daniel a wooden spoon to feign a sword fight while Bekira and I finished packing the baskets. "I think you'll enjoy our weekly outing," Bekira told Daniel. "Levi always guides us to the houses that seem to need bread the most."

I shot an *I told you so* look at my husband. He rolled his eyes but asked, "And you say he's known Eliakim since he was a boy?" A poor attempt at subtlety.

Bekira's smirk proved it. "Has Jerusha convinced you he's an angel?"

"Not yet, but I'd like to spend more time with him and judge for myself."

"Nonsense." Bekira waved off his comment. "Levi and his wife owned the sandal shop in the Lower City when Eliakim's abba was the palace treasurer. Eliakim doesn't remember him, but I'm sure if Hilkiah were still with us, he'd say Levi is a good *man*." Bekira loaded the last loaves into another basket and rested her hands on her ample hips. "I think we're read—"

"Shhh!" Daniel lifted a hand, straining to hear. "Footsteps, running toward—"

Eliakim burst into the main room. "The king is ill." He sorted through the faces in the room and found Bekira's. "He collapsed during this morning's council meeting. One moment he was fine, the next—" Looking up, he blinked rapidly. Sniffed. Controlling his emotions. "The palace physician saw the same illness while training in Egypt." He swallowed hard and let his terrified gaze fall on his wife. "He called it Black Death, Bekira. Thousands died; only one survived."

His face contorted, and she stepped toward him, but he moved back. "No, don't touch me." He lifted the small bag in his hand. "The physician said it may have been caused by the fleas on the scroll delivered by the Assyrian messenger two days ago. He brought Sennacherib's scroll to Hezi from Libnah—from the rat infestation. I've brought more natron powder to sprinkle around our home and in our laundry." He wiped his cheeks and met each one's eyes in the room, switching from husband and abba to efficient administrator. "A carrier pigeon brought word that Assyrians *and* Judeans are dying with the plague in Lachish. Has anyone seen a flea in the house? Daniel, Jerusha—have either of you? Does anyone have suspicious bites or skin irritations?"

"No Abba."

"No, my friend."

Thankfully, everyone shook their heads, and the relief in the room was palpable. "All right," he said, "but no more visits to the Lower City—at least for now."

Bekira pressed both hands against her cheeks. "What about the bread?" Mountains of loaves waited in baskets, the aroma screaming for the hungry souls in need.

"Let me take it to Levi," Daniel said to Eliakim. "I need to feel useful, and I can take one of my carts to deliver it all at once."

Eliakim offered a barely perceptible nod. "You're more than useful, Daniel. You're irreplaceable. So deliver the bread but be sure to return here for some natron to sprinkle on yourself and your clothes before returning home to Jerusha."

The amber reflections of dusk painted the eastern clouds by the time my husband returned from the Lower City. His hair and clothes were wet, smelling of the strong Egyptian cleanser that had become so valuable it was now kept in the palace treasury.

"I've prepared a bath for you," I said when he crossed the threshold. He forced a smile and headed toward the large metal drum I'd borrowed from Bekira. When he untied his belt, I cautioned, "Wait until I add the boiling water."

Something unspoken hung in the air between us. Something neither of us was yet ready to unwrap. Not like a gift tied with colorful ribbons—more like a package in dirty sackcloth found on a doorstep. I poured the large pot of boiling water into the tub while Daniel undressed. He dipped one foot in, then stuffed the rest of himself into the drum, displacing most of the water.

I chuckled and met his gaze. He grinned too, but it faded as his eyes held mine. "We have too much, Jerusha. There are people already starving in the Lower City." Moisture gathered on his lashes. "Levi told me things about those families—about us." He looked down, swiped at his eyes. "If he's not an angel, he's a prophet." He fell silent.

I pursed my lips together, the question clawing to get out. *What did he tell you?* But for some reason, it felt intrusive to ask. My husband would tell me when he was ready. I had news of my own to share, news from Eliakim about our king. Maybe now wasn't the right time. I dipped a cloth into the water and pressed it against his back, letting the warm water soothe before my words scraped his raw emotions.

"Eliakim visited the palace while you were gone but . . ." How could I phrase the news gently?

"Visited the *palace?*" Brow furrowed, he glanced up. "You mean he visited the king?"

Thank You, Yahweh, for opening a path for the hard news. "He wasn't allowed to visit the king." Fear marched across his features. "Isaiah, the prophet, spoke two prophecies over Hezekiah today. In the first, Yahweh decreed Hezekiah would die from his sudden illness."

"What? No!" Daniel's words escaped on a sob.

"But Isaiah barely made it to the Middle Court when Yahweh recanted His judgment." Framing Daniel's face, I whispered, "Yahweh promised to heal our king and gave him fifteen more years of life. Hezekiah will *live*."

Confusion turned to relief that battled again with uncertainty. "How can Yahweh change His mind?"

My hands fell away, and I picked up the cloth again, drawing it across my husband's back. "I've been pondering the same question all afternoon." The gentle splashing accompanied our thoughts in the welcome silence. What were the ramifications of an all-knowing God who might change His plans? If He knew all along that He'd change His mind, had He really changed it? Or was the change not really a change since the change was His original intention? I'd nearly gone mad, tying thoughts into knots.

"Did He change His mind about taking our child?" Daniel asked in barely a whisper.

Yahweh, let it be so. But if He could change His mind for the good . . . "Will He change His mind about saving Jerusalem?" I leaned over to kiss my husband's shoulder, hoping he'd have better answers than me.

"I believe those to be very different questions." He reached for my hand and caught my eye. "God spoke through Isaiah and *promised* Jerusalem's rescue from Assyria. We received no such prophecy or promise about our child, Jerusha."

"Yes, but . . ." I wanted to rant, to stomp my feet and say, *but I want a promise!* Tears clogged my throat, but not my mind. "Don't we have to believe our prayers can move God? If Yahweh isn't swayed by our pleas, what reason is there to pray?"

Daniel drew my fingers to his lips, his eyes narrowed in thought. "What if Yahweh didn't *change* His mind about our baby or the king's life? What if He gave the king—and us—a mountain to climb so our faith muscles could be strengthened for challenges to come?"

I groaned and bowed my head on his shoulder. "Oh, Daniel. I don't want more challenges."

He laid his cheek against it and sighed. "Life is a series of challenges, my love. Haven't we seen God sometimes answer prayer the way we want, and yet other times refuse our requests? But each time we turn to Him, we've learned new things about the Almighty Creator and drawn closer to Him."

I lifted my head and no longer felt the inhibition that kept me silent earlier. "What did Levi tell you today?"

A slow smile appeared on Daniel's handsome face. "He knew I felt safer in the darkness and helped me see it as Yahweh's gift instead of a deficiency. Levi said faith could be easier for me than others who rely on sight because faith is simply being certain of what we can't see—and I've made a life of doing that."

I covered a gasp and then threw my arms around his neck. "It's true!"

In one mischievous moment, strong arms pulled me into the metal tub. We laughed together, ate together, and loved each other long into the night, ignoring the uncertainties tomorrow held.

NINE

"That night the angel of the Lord went out and put to death a hundred and eighty-five thousand in the Assyrian camp. When the people got up the next morning—there were all the dead bodies! So Sennacherib king of Assyria broke camp and withdrew. He returned to Nineveh and stayed there."
2 Kings 19:35-36

DANIEL

The sun was overhead, and Daniel's stomach protested loudly. "At least take some bread with you." Jerusha grabbed a small loaf and ran to meet him at the threshold.

He paused and called to the palace messenger. "I'm coming." Then he took the bread from her hand and bent to kiss her. "What could the king possibly want with me?"

Tears welled in her eyes. "I don't know, but don't get close. And find Eliakim to give you more natron so you don't get sick."

"I'll be fine." He hurried after the messenger. Looking back, he saw Jerusha covering her face, weeping. *Yahweh, give her the assurance You've given me that we'll raise our child together after this nightmare is over.*

"Have you heard the good news?" The messenger asked. Daniel shrugged and fell in step, so the man said, "The king is healed. Lord Isaiah's second prophecy from yesterday seems to be happening."

"Second prophecy?"

"Yes, the miraculous healing that will enable the king to present himself at the Temple within three days."

He neglected to mention that the king was given only fifteen more years to live. "Do you know why he's summoned me?"

"No, my lord, but I suspect it has something to do with Lord Isaiah's prophecy from this morning." The fellow was chattier than most palace couriers.

"I've not heard about that prophecy."

"He said the Assyrians are dead, my lord."

"What Assyrians?" Daniel shot a disbelieving stare at the man.

"The ones outside our walls, my lord."

It couldn't be. "All of them?"

"That's what Lord Isaiah told the queen when she visited him this morning."

Madness. How could an entire army die overnight? *I should have looked out our window this morning.*

The messenger led Daniel up the palace stairs, into the public entrance, and then down a private hallway. The mosaic-tiled floor boasted brilliant images of lions and eagles, representing the tribe of Judah and her king. Lush tapestries graced the walls, and expensive pottery was displayed atop tables inlaid with ebony and ivory. Daniel clasped his hands in front of him so he wouldn't accidentally break something. Near the end of the long hall stood four of the king's guard at a double-doored chamber—the king's, he presumed.

Suddenly nervous, Daniel slowed his pace. "Are you sure the

king is ready to receive me? Wasn't he near death only last night?"

The messenger stopped only a few paces from the royal guards at King Hezekiah's door. "I left this chamber only moments before arriving at your home. The king was sitting on a couch with Queen Hephzibah, enjoying candied dates and fruit juice while his wife played the lyre. The king sent me to fetch you and another messenger to summon Lord Eliakim. I suspect they're waiting for us." He extended his hand toward the chamber and bowed slightly, waiting for me to gather my courage and complete our journey.

I hesitated, but the guards opened the doors, leaving me no choice. The king, queen, and Eliakim stood just over the threshold and looked my way—all appearing weary but healthy.

"Daniel! Come and join us." The king lifted his silver goblet. "Fresh pomegranate juice will cure anything that ails you."

The queen nudged his shoulder. "We all know *Yahweh* healed you."

"Indeed he did." The king lifted his face to heaven. "May all praise and honor be Yahweh's forever and ever."

"Amen!" Daniel joined the chorus and entered the chamber, feeling the camaraderie of the faithful. Bowing to his king, he was surprised by overwhelming emotion. "I can't tell you how happy I am that you are well, my king. Your righteous reign is the life blood of Judah's rescue."

He felt a hand on his shoulder and stood, meeting the king's intense gaze. "It is not my righteousness that saved us, Daniel, but God's rich mercy."

Daniel went to one knee. "How may I serve you, my king?"

"Follow me to the balcony, my friend," he said, patting Daniel's shoulder again. "There's something you should see."

He stood and gave Eliakim a quizzical look as they fell in step together, following the king and queen. His friend's brows rose, and he shook his head. "Prepare yourself, my friend. I've seen it, and I still can't believe it."

We stepped onto the balcony, and I followed the royal couple to its edge, where King Hezekiah swept his arm in the direction of the Kidron Valley below. My mouth fell open at the sight. Carrion birds littered the Assyrian camp below, tearing at the flesh of an enemy we'd feared for centuries.

"All of them?" I could manage only a croak.

The king sighed. "Commander Jokim believes a few escaped before dawn in the direction of Lachish, but we've just received a message on carrier pigeon—which is why I sent for you."

The odd comment snapped Daniel from his stupor. "What could this have to do with me?"

"My brother, Mattaniah, sent word that the Assyrians retreated from Lachish when they heard of the total devastation in Jerusalem. King Sennacherib has *returned the way he came*." Hezekiah emphasized Isaiah's prophecy. "But Lachish is overrun with dead bodies. Dead Assyrians lay outside its walls, and Judeans judged for their idolatry are stacked inside the city in piles as high as the walls. We need Judah's Mole to dig a grave large enough to bury them all."

A thousand questions raced through Daniel's mind. "Where will we bury Jerusalem's dead Assyrians, my king?"

"We'll burn them," he said without hesitation. "In the Valley of Ben Hinnom, where pagans have sacrificed to their idols for generations."

"A fitting end." Daniel inclined his head in respect. His second question was less practical but just as important. "If I may, my king, how many died in Jerusalem as judgment for idolatry?" He'd heard rumors of those who maintained the pagan practices begun by Hezekiah's abba, King Ahaz.

"None." The king gathered his queen under his arm. They gazed at each other as he explained. "Isaiah seems to think that I was afflicted for our city's iniquities. Though he once thought I was punished for my mistakes, he now believes the punishment

I bore brought our city peace. That by my wounds, Jerusalem was healed."

The queen brushed her husband's cheek, and Daniel felt as if he intruded on a holy moment between them. But she quickly returned her focus to Daniel. "We believe my husband is but a whisper of the Savior promised by Yahweh. Hezi is *a* son of David and a righteous king, but the true Savior in my abba's prophecies will heal every wound and bring salvation to all."

Daniel stood in awe of the royal couple before him. He still had questions about the task he'd been given, but all else paled in comparison to the truth he'd just heard. "May our Savior come quickly, my queen." He bowed, closing his eyes to let his senses come alive. The smell of death. The sounds of a city coming back to life. And his faith awakening to the promises he couldn't see but believed with more certainty than the light of day.

Authors Note

I hope you enjoyed *The Mole's Wife* and "seeing" Hezekiah's Tunnel come to life in your imagination—as it has in my mind for many years! You can read the *Truth* of King Hezekiah's reign and the Assyrian attack on Jerusalem in 2 Kings 18-20 and 2 Chronicles 29-32. But facts and fiction get a little blurred when experts offer multiple opinions on archaeological findings and ancient research. When writing a biblical novel, my job is to find a golden thread amid the differing scholarly opinions and tie it together with the absolute Truth of God's Word. I then use shades of creative fiction to make the picture look as complete—and seamless—as possible.

So was there a fella called "Judah's Mole?" Nope, totally my imagination. However, there is a tunnel that connected the Gihon Spring with a cistern within what is now called "The Old City" in Jerusalem, and it shows *evidence* that diggers started from both sides of the mountain and met in the middle!

The Gihon Spring is thought to be associated with the water shaft used by David to conquer the city when the Jebusites boasted that "even the blind and lame" could ward him off.

> *"On that day David had said, 'Anyone who conquers the Jebusites will have to use the water shaft to reach those "lame and blind" who are David's enemies.' That is why they say, 'The "blind and lame" will not enter the palace.'"*
> **2 Samuel 5:8**

> *"As for the other events of Hezekiah's reign, all his achievements and how he made the pool and the tunnel by which he brought water into the city, are they not written in the book of the annals of the kings of Judah?"*
> **2 Kings 20:20**

It was fun to revisit some of my favorite characters: Hezi, Zibah, and Eliakim. And I really enjoyed giving Eliakim a sassy wife and three children. I purposely left you wondering about Levi. Was he an angel? A prophet? Though I don't give a lot of thought to angels, I do appreciate the New Testament command:

> *"Do not forget to show hospitality to strangers, for by so doing some people have shown hospitality to angels without knowing it."*
> **Hebrews 13:2**

Was there a mass grave in Lachish where archaeologists discovered countless Assyrian arrowheads and the remains of 1,500 people? Absolutely! And, interestingly—the bones they found had no evidence of wounds (nicks), which indicated illness rather than torture as cause of death. (To find out more, check out: http://bit.ly/LachishGrave)

To create a short story around the biblical events, we need only remember that God's Word records His-story (history)—but not EVERYONE'S story. There were thousands of people in Jerusalem who knew nothing of palace events, people like you and me, who weren't part of the noble class. They still experienced fear, uncertainty, and then the ultimate victory of the miraculous events we read about in God's Word.

I trust reading *The Mole's Wife* gives you hope and certainty that the same God, who did unseen things inside ancient Israel's highest echelons of government, continues His work in the world's nations—and us—today. Though our world can feel out of control, the same sovereign Creator can empower His people with miraculous skill and mustard-seed faith to stand against impossible odds.

Thanks for reading!

About the Author

MESU ANDREWS is a Christy Award-winning, best-selling author of biblical novels and devotional studies whose deep understanding of and love for God's Word brings the Bible alive for readers. Her heritage as a "spiritual mutt" has given her a strong yearning to both understand and communicate biblical truths in powerful stories that touch the heart, challenge the mind, and transform lives. Mesu lives in Indiana with her husband Roy, where she stays connected with her readers through newsie emails, blog posts, and the social media we all love to hate. For more information, visit MesuAndrews.com.

Also by Mesu Andrews

FICTION TITLES

The Edge of Promise

Beauty's Surrender

In Feast or Famine

Potiphar's Wife

Reluctant Rival

Prophets & Kings

Isaiah's Legacy

Of Fire and Lions

By the Waters of Babylon

Isaiah's Daughter

Miriam

Pharaoh's Daughter

In the Shadow of Jezebel

Love in a Broken Vessel

Love's Sacred Song

Love Amid the Ashes

NON-FICTION TITLES

Deep-O-Tionals - Genesis: Part 1

Deep-O-Tionals - Genesis: Part 2

Deep-O-Tionals - Genesis: Part 3

Egyptian Chronicles

Joseph, sold by his brothers and betrayed by Potiphar's wife, is redeemed by interpreting a young pharaoh's dreams. Promoted to Egypt's second-highest office, Joseph must shepherd the whole nation through fourteen years of feast and famine—while navigating a marriage to Asenath, the pagan priestess Pharaoh gives him.

Abandoned. Rejected. Humiliated. One woman trapped in her Egyptian marriage longs to be free—and is willing to betray Joseph, her husband's good and godly servant, to do it.

Meet the pagan priest's daughter, who marries Joseph to change him, but later discovers she's part of Elohim's plan to change the world.

Available wherever books are sold

Prophets and Kings

Hephzibah is taken captive then marries her lifelong love, King Hezekiah. But when the fulfillment of the prophecy of her father, Isaiah, puts her son, King Manasseh, on Judah's throne, the repercussions of Manasseh's evil deeds echo for generations, leading to Daniel and his friends' exile to Babylon.

Follow the story of Hephzibah, from captive to queen, as she learns to trust Yahweh and the people He chose to love her.

Follow King Hezekiah and Queen Hephzibah's story through their son, King Manasseh, and witness Yahweh's power to redeem the evilest prodigal of all.

Experience the familiar stories of Daniel, Shadrach, Meshach, and Abednego through the eyes of Daniel's fictional wife and see Yahweh's power at work in world history.

Available wherever books are sold

Treasures of the Nile

Pharaoh's daughter dares to defy the gods, drawing a Hebrew baby from the Nile and making the boy a prince of Egypt. Meet the prince, Moses, after he's exiled to Midian and returns to Egypt as an eighty-year-old man—and experience Israel's Exodus through his sister Miriam's eyes.

Pharaoh's Daughter—the sister of King Tut—draws a Hebrew boy from the Nile and changes not only her life with her defiance but the future of nations.

See the Exodus through Miriam's eighty-six-year-old eyes. Having known only a life of slavery and the God named Elohim, how can Miriam accept her younger brother, Moses, who returns to Egypt after forty years, promising Israel's freedom and touting God's new name?

Available wherever books are sold

Printed in Great Britain
by Amazon